YEAR ONE
Marooned!

BRAD STRICKLAND and THOMAS E. FULLER

Aladdin Paperbacks
New York   London   Toronto   Sydney

To Diane

Thanks to Ron Butler for his technical and scientific advice

First Aladdin Paperbacks edition June 2004

Copyright © 2004 by Brad Strickland and the Estate of Thomas E. Fuller

ALADDIN PAPERBACKS
An imprint of Simon & Schuster
Children's Publishing Division
1230 Avenue of the Americas
New York, NY 10020

Printed in the United States of America

10 9 8 7 6 5 4 3 2 1

The Library of Congress Control Number 2003096184
ISBN 0-689-86400-0

1.1

"If you forget everything else, remember the most important fact about this planet: Mars has a million ways to kill you."

Lieutenant Mpondo swept his gaze over the twenty new arrivals. Sean Doe, in the fourth and last row, met his dark brown eyes without smiling, nodding, or blinking. Sean was over fifteen years old, and for most of that time people had been trying to kill him.

Sean and the nineteen others—all of them adults—sat strapped in, since the *Argosy* was still in space and they were weightless. Mpondo, a man of twenty-five with his hair cropped to a shadow on his skull, hovered with his feet just off the deck, a wall belt looped around his waist to keep him from drifting. He wore the orange uniform of the Interplanetary Service. It was the worse for wear, but after more than a year of traveling, the same could be said for everyone's clothes. Mpondo opened a panel and pressed a button, and the viewport, a ten-foot square 3-D screen, cleared to give them a view of space.

And of Mars, closer than ever before.

The ruddy reddish-orange disk nearly filled the viewport. The hemisphere of the planet that Sean could see lay in full sunlight. Mars looked like a ravaged world, all her blemishes showing: long shadowed cracks that were really canyons deeper than any on Earth, impact craters, a south pole ringed with an icy white cap, blurred haze. Someone in the front row murmured and pointed as a falling meteorite sketched a brilliant line across the planet near the polar ice cap.

"Just a delivery," Mpondo said in a loud voice. "That's ice, coming in from the robot mass driver on Jupiter's moon Ganymede. Approximately twice a day the mass driver fires a projectile of compacted ice in an orbit that whips it around Jupiter and sends it to Mars. After a journey of years, the projectile comes into the Martian atmosphere within twenty degrees of the south pole—yes?"

A man in the row ahead of Sean had his hand up. "How big are these things?" he asked.

"On Earth they would mass about twenty-five tons," Mpondo replied, looking mildly irritated at the interruption. "And to answer your next question, they pose no threat to Marsport. They don't come anywhere near the base. Their orbits bring them in at a shallow angle over the south polar regions, where they mostly evaporate—because of the heat of entering the atmosphere—before they even reach the surface. They've been crashing into the Martian atmosphere for more than thirty years now, adding water, carbon dioxide, and other gases to the planet. As a result, the Martian air is growing denser. One day it will be rich enough in oxygen to allow you to breathe on the surface, and thick enough to hold the sun's heat. But that day's a long time off."

Sean could make out cloud patterns in the atmosphere of Mars, swirls and sweeps of pale color, and he noticed now how the edges of the planet blurred to blue haze against the darkness of space, unlike the sharp lines of Luna, the Earth's airless moon, where he had trained for the trip to Mars.

Mpondo was holding up a finger. "Right now, if you tried to breathe the atmosphere on Mars, it would kill you." He held up another finger. "Right now, if you took an unprotected stroll outside of Marsport, you would freeze to death. Right now, if Marsport didn't receive regular resupply from Earth, the colonists would starve. I could go on, but I think that makes the point. Mars is a deadly world."

A new world, though, Sean thought. He felt strange just contemplating his trip—no, his escape—from Earth. His chest tingled as he reflected on being among the first humans to live on a different planet from Earth, from the homeworld. So Mars was deadly? So what? Bring it on.

Sean could not remember his parents. He could barely remember his rescue. He was one of a dozen survivors of the Aberlin tragedy, an act of biological terrorism that had erased a small Scottish town from existence. They told him he had been two when the attack happened. He vaguely remembered the American team that had found him and had flown him, isolated, across the Atlantic.

He remembered the endless stream of doctors who had jabbed and bled him, X-rayed and imaged him, tested and prodded and poked him, trying to learn why he had lived when hundreds of others had died. He was a specimen to them, nothing more.

Sean supposed he had been about eight years old when a court had ordered his release. That's when he had been given a name. Previously he had been AVS-3, Aberlin Village Survivor Three. The American media had decided to call him

John Doe. When he had learned what that meant, a generic term for an unknown, he had changed it just enough to make it his own: "Sean" was Scottish for "John," and so he had become Sean Doe.

The government had placed him in a foster home, and within a month he had escaped from it. For three years he had survived in the urban jungle of Deep New York, where gangs of young thugs faced down everything law enforcers could throw at them. And he had survived.

At eleven, he was illiterate, underweight, and sick with half a dozen diseases of poverty. Then Dr. Simak had tracked him down at last.

Of all the doctors who had examined him, Dr. Amanda Simak was the only one that Sean had halfway trusted. And, as it turned out, she was the only one who seemed to care whether AVS-3 lived or died. She had found him in a burned-out storefront, wounded and ill, and had taken him, not to a hospital or to an institution, but to her home. She had treated his wounds and his sicknesses, had taught him to read, had learned how intelligent he was. More importantly to Sean, she had legally adopted him.

All in one year.

Sean could remember that period of seventeen months, from the middle of his eleventh year to his thirteenth, as an interval of security in a life of danger. For the first time in his life, no one had been trying to hurt him. For the first time in his life, he had trusted an adult.

And then she had broken the news one morning while they sat on a jumble of boulders overlooking the stream that flowed near her home in the mountains. "Sean, I'm going away."

He had not protested, and he had not cried. He had never cried in his life. "Where?"

She had pointed up into the blue sky of Earth and smiled. Amanda Simak was forty-two, a tall woman, with light brown hair and a plain, thin face made lively by the bluest eyes Sean had ever seen. "Mars."

"Take me."

She had shaken her head. "Not yet. You're too young. But when the time comes—"

"What will happen to me?"

She took one of his hands. "Not another foster home. I have friends who live in Florida. That's very different from here, but I think you'll like it. The Marsport Commission has agreed to consider sending young people to the colony, but that's in the future. When you can come, I'll send for you."

And that was that. The couple in Florida, the Thomases, were much younger than Dr. Simak, and they tried their best. Sean learned to swim in the sea, and to fish and sail. They worried because he never laughed, never cried, never showed any sign of temper.

But they didn't realize how little they knew about what he was feeling. Sean had a gift he could not explain or fully understand. It was a mental ability to put together trends, facts, and forces and predict what would happen.

He watched the news and studied history. He learned of the forces in Old Europe, South America, Central Asia, Africa, all warring for their rights, their wishes, their desires.

In his head, lines of force intersected, changed direction, grew more intense.

And Sean knew something would happen in three to five years. Something terrible.

He never spoke of it. After Dr. Simak had arrived to take charge of Marsport, he never told even her. Their communication was odd, to be sure. Mars was so far from Earth that it took half an hour or more for transmissions to travel from one planet to the next. Instead of conversations, they had a series of monologues. Dr. Simak would appear on the monitor, smiling, saying, "Hello, Sean. Here's the news from Mars," and then would talk for ten or fifteen minutes. When she had finished, Sean would reply for about the same length of time, then transmit.

And in thirty or forty minutes, she would get his reply.

But he never told her what he saw coming.

They had been apart for well over a year when she sent word at last: "You can come." He traveled to Luna, Earth's moon. The colonists there called their underground warren "Lunacy," and they called themselves "Lunatics," but always with a grin. They had given Sean a crash course in Martian survival, and they had seen him aboard the *Argosy* for the long trip through space. Sean had never once complained.

By then he knew, although he could not quite express how he knew, that for Earth, time was running out.

1.3

The *Argosy* went into orbit a hundred miles above the surface of Mars. The new colonists flew down to Marsport in three landers sent up from the surface, each able to carry only six passengers. Sean's chance did not come until the last day, when he and five others were cleared for landing. He never got a clear glimpse of the lander he was boarding, but from his training back on Luna he knew that it was shaped something like a flattened cone.

He had a window seat, and he stared out of a very small viewport as the craft dropped into the upper reaches of the Martian atmosphere. The lander turned, coming in tail-first at this altitude. Turbulence jolted and jarred him, and he heard the other colonists murmuring in tones of worry, but he held on and stared out the window. The distant landscape gradually grew closer and more distinct until they were sweeping over a chaotic world of craters, boulders, vast gullies, and wind-whipped sheets of sand.

Then the lander rotated, and Sean caught his breath. He could see the immense dome of a mountain, one far larger than any on Earth: Olympus Mons, an enormous dead volcano that towered fifteen miles high.

Somewhere at its base was Marsport.

It took the lander another hour to pass over the gigantic mountain and touch down on a landing pad, a stretch of bare red rock that had been scraped smooth. The return of gravity, even the weak gravity of Mars, felt strange to Sean. Like everyone else on the *Argosy,* Sean had put in several hours a week in the centrifuge, a rotating cylinder that gave the effect of gravity. That was necessary because being too long in weightlessness tended to weaken a person's bones and circulatory system. Still, that had been temporary and artificial. Now, as he stood up from his seat, Sean felt the tug of a planet again. On Earth he had weighed a little over one hundred pounds. Here it was more like forty-three, but after the weightlessness of space, he felt as if he were wading through molasses.

The passengers filed forward through a hatch into a sealed disembarkation tube, a long, slanting ramp without windows. At the far end was a corridor lighted by fluorescent panels, and at the end of the corridor Sean stepped into a dome that gave him a sense of spaciousness.

It was thirty meters—about a hundred feet—in diameter. And two-thirds of its walls were viewscreens.

He nearly bounced as he made his way over to look out of one of the screens—getting back the habit of walking properly was difficult. He steadied himself and stared out at the Martian plain. He had expected a pink sky, but it was blue; a deep, clear blue. Some distance away, a rugged cliff rose up and up, and beyond that were the slopes of Olympus Mons itself. Sean felt a little drop of disappointment. The mountain was so far away and so vast that it faded into a purple, hazy blur. He wasn't even sure that he could see the summit—

"Sean."

He turned at once and felt his throat tighten.

Dr. Simak stood a few feet away. She was wearing a light gray tunic with pockets everywhere, darker gray slacks, and black boots. Her lined face was smiling, and her blue eyes gleamed with tears. "I've waited a long time to see you again."

Sean lurched toward her, nearly falling. He hugged her tightly. "I'm glad to be here," he said, his voice a rough whisper.

1.4

Sean shifted in his seat. He had been on Mars for less than an hour, and now he was waiting with the other newcomers in a classroom for an orientation session.

A blond girl wandered in, spotted him as the only teen in the whole group, and came to sit beside him, making herself right at home. "Jenny Laslo," the girl said, offering her hand. As Sean shook it, she frowned and asked, "What kind of outfit is that?"

"It's mine," Sean said, surprised. He was wearing a dark blue V-neck shirt, baggy trousers, sneakers, and over it all his favorite leather jacket, black and very long so that it hung to his knees. Jenny, he noticed, was wearing the standard gray tunic, black slacks, and boots. He frowned. "What's wrong with my clothes?"

"Well, nothing. They're just a little unusual. Not that we have a uniform or anything. So who are you?"

"Sean Doe."

Jenny's eyes, which were a light blue, widened. "*The* Sean Doe? The one Dr. Simak adopted?"

"Yes," Sean said shortly. He dreaded the questions that would come next, about his real parents and how he had lost them.

"Ice," Jenny said.

"What?"

"Ice," she repeated. "You know—the coolest. She's a great person. So what's your specialty?"

Sean shook his head. "I don't have a specialty," Sean said.

"You'll get one. Me, I'm in adaptive agriculture. You know, studying how plants and animals adapt to nonterrestrial conditions. I'll introduce you to the rest of the brat squad later. First you have to do the 'Mars will kill you' bit."

"Done it already," Sean told her. "Lieutenant Mpondo on the *Argosy*. Twenty lectures, all of them winding up by reminding us that Mars wants us dead."

Jenny tilted her head. "No, it doesn't. It doesn't care, that's all. Remember that, and you've got the most important thing spiked from the beginning. Mars doesn't hate you. It just never forgives a mistake. Simple, right?"

Some of the adults who had made the flight with Sean came in and found places near the front of the classroom. Jenny jerked her head toward the door. "Ax the class. You don't need it if you're not specializing yet."

Sean had been wondering how he was going to cope with another round of information about all the dangers of Mars. He grinned. "Okay."

The two of them walked out with considerably more grace than the adults who were shuffling down the corridor holding on to wall rails as they tried to readjust to gravity. Sean followed Jenny down a maze of passageways. She seemed to know everyone they passed, and they all spoke to her. She finally led Sean into the biggest dome he had seen, this one a clear greenhouse more than two hundred meters across. Jenny was grinning at him. "This is ice. Well, it's water, not ice, but it's the coolest. Lake Ares."

For a few seconds Sean wasn't quite sure what he was seeing, and then everything clicked. "It's a crater," he said.

They stood on the edge of a body of water so calm that it looked like a sheet of glass. It was almost perfectly round. The afternoon sunlight slanting in glistened on its surface, making it a blue shimmer. "It's the only body of water on Mars," Jenny said.

"Maybe one day they'll let us swim in it. Meanwhile, it's got a few fish and a great way of splashing." She sat at the edge of the water, swept a hand down and slapped the surface.

In the low gravity, a spray of water rose into the air, then fell as if in slow motion. Undulating waves broke out on the surface of the lake, rolling across the water in lazy expanding circles. "Where does this come from?" Sean asked.

"Ice mines," Jenny responded. "Well, not really, but that's what we call them. Mars has a pretty good store of permafrost—water that's under the surface and permanently frozen. When Olympus was erupting, it shot out a lot of water vapor. That condensed and fell as rain—the atmosphere used to be thick enough for that—and the water seeped down underground. When the first engineers were making the tunnels, they hit pockets of permafrost. Later, when the Marsport project started, some of them domed in this crater and began melting the permafrost and pumping the water in to create this reservoir. It's more than thirty meters deep at the center. We haven't had to draw on it for drinking water yet. We probably will soon, because the permafrost that's within reach is about played out."

Sean watched as the slow-motion waves reached the far shore, then rebounded, coming back their way. "What about the ice at the South Pole?"

"The meteorites, you mean?" Jenny shrugged. "That's mostly for the sake of the atmosphere. As the meteorites evaporate, they add water vapor, nitrogen, oxygen, and carbon dioxide to the air. You know the air pressure today is thirty times what it was in 2050? In some of the rifts, the pressure's up to three hundred millibars, but that's still not much. Maybe you know that on Earth, standard sea-level pressure is one thousand thirteen millibars. Still, we get clouds all the time now. Maybe in fifty more years we'll get rain. Or snow."

Sean stared out at the surface. Long shadows were creeping across the rusty red plain. The afternoon sun shone on a complex of domes, towers, and antennae. A half-dozen people in pressure suits were working out there, clearing boulders from a stretch of ground between the dome Sean and Jenny stood in and the next one. "When do we get out?" Sean asked.

"Oh, you won't be able to go outside for a couple of weeks," Jenny said. "Not until you learn all about the dangers of the surface. But you can sum them up pretty easily."

"I know," Sean replied solemnly. "Mars has a million ways to kill you."

They looked solemnly at each other for ten seconds. Then Jenny began to laugh, and to his own astonishment, Sean joined in. Like gravity, laughing felt very strange. Good, but very strange indeed.

CHAPTER 2

"What are you doing here?"

The voice startled Sean, and he turned quickly—too quickly in the low gravity of Mars. He couldn't stop and went sprawling onto the sandy edge of the lake. He scrambled up, teetering for balance, and fell forward again—into the arms of an angry-looking man, who set him on his feet.

Jenny was speaking fast in an anxious tone. "We weren't doing anything, Dr. Ellman. Sean's new, and I was just showing him—"

Ellman was a heavyset man in his thirties, with black hair cut close to his head. Everything about him was square: his broad shoulders, his thick body, his heavy chin. He scowled at both of them from dark eyes set deeply under heavy brows. "If he's new, he should be at the Asimov Project orientation. What's the name?"

"Sean Doe," Sean said, meeting the man's unpleasant gaze.

A smile that looked more like a sneer crinkled its way across Ellman's lips. "Yes," he said. "I've heard of Sean Doe. The ward of Dr. Simak, I believe. She will not be pleased to hear how you're beginning your stay on Mars, Doe. Or how Laslo here is contributing to your rule-breaking."

"It isn't her fault," Sean said. "It's just that I've heard these lectures before, and I asked her—"

"Heard them before?" Ellman cut in. "Oh, so you can read minds, can you? You're sure that you know everything that can possibly be presented to you? Tell me, if you're so certain, how much of our power is provided by areothermal wells and how much by wind generation?"

Sean stared stupidly at him. "I—uh, I don't know."

"No. How many kilometers of lava tubes have we adapted for storage, power generation, and factory space?"

Heat crept upward from Sean's throat into his face. He tried to control his anger at these unfair questions and merely shook his head.

"Is that an answer, Doe?" snapped Ellman.

"No, sir," Sean said. "I don't know."

"We have 3,212 colonists at the present time. At a standard rate of consumption, disregarding recycling, how many months' water supply do we have?"

Jenny whispered, "Six."

But Ellman whipped his head toward her. "I heard that, Laslo! You're confined to quarters for the rest of the day. Doe, come with me."

Sean gave Jenny a helpless look, and she shrugged an apology. The three of them traveled down a corridor to an intersection, where Jenny split off to the left. Ellman said, "I suppose you know about the color-coded doors, Mr. Doe?"

That was a question Sean could answer. It had been part of the training on Luna. "A red-coded door means the room has an opening onto the

Martian surface," he said. "If the room loses pressure, there's no way anyone could survive inside. A yellow-coded door doesn't have a wall that adjoins the surface, but no resupply of air. If there's a breach to the surface, the room will hold air and anyone in it would be safe for as long as the air held out. A green door means the room has a constant supply of—"

"At least you know something."

Sean plowed on., "The doors don't open automatically because they have to be heavy in case of a pressure loss, and the power needed to open and close them—"

"When I want to know that, I'll ask you," snapped Ellman. He marched Sean for what seemed like miles until they came to a dome with a sign reading ADMINISTRATION above the entrance. Around the perimeter six doors were arranged. Ellman made for the one farthest from the entrance to the dome and pressed his hand against a plate beside the door.

It opened, and they stepped into a small office.

Amanda Simak sat at a desk studying a holographic projection that hovered above her computer console. "Yes?" she asked without looking away.

"This young man has committed a serious breach of the rules," Ellman said stiffly.

Amanda looked up, her expression stern. It changed to one of surprise when she saw who the culprit was. "Sean? What's he done?"

Ellman explained, making it seem as if cutting a lecture was the equivalent of armed robbery. When he finished, he added, "I'd suggest confinement for at least a week."

Amanda nodded grimly. "I will consider your suggestion, Dr. Ellman. Thank you. You may leave us alone now."

With a final scowl at Sean, Ellman turned and strode from the office. As soon as the door had closed behind him, Sean said, "I didn't mean to cause any trouble—"

Amanda shook her head. "Of course not. But you've had lectures enough to last a lifetime on the trip from Earth. I know." She touched a pad near her computer and the holographic display—a maze of red and green corridors connecting red and green domes—faded. Another touch of the pad, and a section of the wall behind her cleared, becoming a window looking out onto the afternoon landscape of Mars. Long shadows stretched away, twinkling with frost.

"That's what interests you. A new world."

Sean nodded. "I met a girl, and she was going to show me around."

"What girl?"

"Her name is Jenny. Jenny Laslo."

Amanda smiled. "Yes, she's one for bending the rules herself. Sit down, Sean."

Sean sat in the only other chair in the office, on the other side of the desk from Amanda. She sighed. "Well, we won't be too harsh on this first day. However, you will have to cooperate, Sean. I don't know if you're aware of how controversial the Asimov Project is."

Sean shrugged. "It's just a few teenagers."

"More than that," Amanda told him. "Twenty young people, between the ages of thirteen and eighteen. You got the very last spot in the project, Sean. You should know that there are many on Earth who say that the dangers we face are too great to allow us to risk the lives of young people. Others say the whole effort is a waste and that Mars can never be a home to humans, so sending anyone here, let alone youngsters, is futile. We intend to prove the doubters wrong. The purpose of Marsport is to test whether Mars can ever be fully colonized by humans. Our task is to prove that we can survive for one Martian year—do you know how long that is?"

"Six hundred and eighty-seven Earth days," Sean said. It was a figure he had heard over and over during the long voyage from Earth.

Amanda nodded. "Very close. Actually, 686.98 Earth days. The Martian day is a little longer than an Earth one—24 hours and 37 minutes, approximately—so in Martian terms, the Martian year is 651.17 days long.

That's a long time, Sean. A very long time for a colony to be independent from Earth."

She put her hands together, making a steeple of her fingertips. "We believe that the Martian colony has to reflect a real community, just as the lunar colony now does. A real community includes teenagers and even children. The Asimov Project is very expensive, Sean. That's why the selection process was so difficult. And that's another reason people on Earth object. For what it cost to send you to Mars, the Levelers say, a thousand poor children on Earth could be fed, clothed, and housed for a year."

Sean shook his head. "There'd be no point. Things are falling apart on Earth."

"I know they are," Amanda said. "The trouble is that the governments of Earth are too stubborn to admit it." She rose from behind her desk. "All right. You have to learn to live with rules, Sean. Dr. Ellman isn't very diplomatic, but he's right about some things. Do you understand?"

"I guess so," Sean said. "It's just that—well, I've

been on my own for so long. But I'll try. And I'll take my punishment."

Amanda looked satisfied. "I appreciate that attitude. Confinement to your dormitory wing for the remainder of the day and night. And tomorrow you will attend the orientation sessions. Is that clear?"

"Yes."

"You're dismissed."

It wasn't quite so simple. Marsport seemed vast and confusing, and finally Amanda walked with Sean to the same intersection where Jenny had turned away. "Your dormitory section is to the right," Amanda said. "Your room is A4-5. That's Asimov section, fourth group, fifth room. Clear?"

Sean glanced at her. "A green-coded door," he said.

Amanda gave him an odd look. "Yes, it is. All the dormitories are green-coded. Anyway, your luggage should be there already. Better hurry, or you'll miss your dinner."

Sean made his way down another corridor. He could hear voices from ahead. He opened the heavy green-banded door and stepped into an open area ten feet across and thirty feet long. Four teenagers sat at a table, eating and talking. They fell silent when he stepped in. One of them rose and gave him a brilliant smile. "Sean Doe, I'll bet! Your travel case showed up half an hour ago. We've already gone through it." He grinned. "Just kidding. But we're supposed to expect a Sean Doe, and you must be him."

Sean nodded, uneasy to be meeting these new people.

The boy who had spoken was African, perhaps one year younger than Sean. He was slim, a little shorter than Sean, and quick in his movements. "Grab some chow and sit down! I'll introduce your cellmates! I'll start with me, since I'm the leader."

The others jeered him good-naturedly. "Okay, okay," he said, still smiling as he sat down again. "I am only a legend in my own mind. I'm Alex Benford, and one day I'm going to be the hottest pilot on Mars."

"Uh, glad to meet you," Sean said. "But where's the food?"

"New man! New man!" said an Asian youth. He jumped up. "Come this way, Sean, and I'll show you. And don't let Alex fool you. I'm the oldest, so I'm the leader of this crew. My name's Patrick Nakoma, I'm eighteen—the old man of the Asimov Project, thank you very much—and I'm in zoology. That means I help take care of the animals we're trying to adapt to Mars. Here we go, this is the mess module."

Sean realized that this area was almost exactly like the Administration dome—a large central space with rooms opening off it—and followed Patrick into a hexagonal room. "Here you go," Patrick said, opening a panel in the wall and pulling out a tray. "This is the food. Pop it in here." He slid the tray into another panel and in ten seconds it popped back out again. "Now it's cooked. Utensils are here." He opened still another panel and produced a knife, fork, and spoon. "Glasses are here, and this dispenses your drink. Today it's synthetic chocolate milk, water, or lemonade."

Sean chose the chocolate milk and took his tray back to the table. Patrick showed him how the lid lifted off and folded under. The meal was chicken, vegetables, and a roll. Sean's mouth began to water at the aroma, and he dug in as Alex continued. "Before I was rudely interrupted by Mr. Nakoma there—aren't you retiring next year, old man?—I was about to introduce your other two dorm mates. On your left is the youngest human being on the entire planet, Master Roger Smith."

"I'm thirteen," objected Roger, his accent revealing him to be British. He had untidy brown hair—long for a colonist—a snub nose, and a pale complexion. "That means I'm only a year younger than Alex, so pay no attention to him. I'm pre-engineering."

"Watch out for Roger," Alex warned as Sean wolfed down his food. "He's got a warped sense of humor. And last and certainly least, on your right is Mr. Michael Goldberg, another old codger. What are you, Mickey, seventy-one?"

"Seventeen," Mickey corrected. He had a plump face, curly dark hair, and—most unusually—round rimless glasses. "Hydraulics specialist. And before you ask, I can't have corrective surgery and I hate contact lenses, so I wear specs. What's your specialty, Sean?"

Sean gulped some synthetic chocolate milk, which tasted almost completely unlike real chocolate milk. "Don't have one yet," he said.

They waited for a moment, and then Alex asked, "How old are you?"

"Fifteen and six months," Sean replied.

"And how many days?" Roger asked with a grin.

"No, I'm just joking with you. Go ahead and eat. You look starved."

Though he had shown up late, Sean was so hungry that he finished his dinner along with the others. They showed him how to return the tray to yet another compartment for washing, then explained the layout.

"Bathroom and shower are in the module to the right of the mess module," Alex said. "Computer library and rec module is the one to the left. Then our rooms, which I'm sure you're going to love just as much as we do. Patrick's in number one, because he showed up first. Then Mickey in two, me in three, and Roger in four. Yours is five, right over there. And the last one, in case you're interested, is the laundry. We do our own. Oh, what we sacrifice to be a part of the Asimov Project!"

The room wasn't very impressive, Sean had to admit. It was hexagonal, like all the others, and was perhaps eight feet in diameter. The desk, with its own small computer, was beside the door. The chair folded out from the wall. Storage shelves occupied three of the other five walls. One wall was actually a closet door—he unpacked his clothes and hung them there—and the last one folded down to become a bed.

The others were playing some complex computer game in the common room and invited him to join them, but he begged off, explaining that he was tired. "Anyway, I'd better go to my room," he finished. "I'm sort of confined to quarters."

"Why?" Roger asked, sounding surprised.

Sean explained the trouble he had landed in. The others looked at each other, shaking their heads. "Man, you got off on the wrong foot," Alex said sympathetically. "Ellman's a real pain. You have to watch out for him, or you'll be on the first shuttle back to TF."

"TF?" Sean asked.

"Terra firma," Mickey explained. "Otherwise known as Earth. Ellman's a stickler for rules."

"Most of which he makes up on the spot," Patrick put in. "That's just to keep us on our toes."

"I'm terrified of him," Roger said.

Sean stared at the younger boy. "Really?"

"Well," Roger said with a grin, "at least I'm always sure to leave no clues when I pull something on him. Seriously, though, Ellman hates the Asimov Project. I think he's secretly a Leveler."

"I hate Levelers," Sean said.

"I think they're a bunch of nuts who just think they're important," Mickey added with a shrug.

"Besides," Roger said with a grin, "what did they ever do to you?"

"They killed my parents," Sean said evenly. "I was born in Aberlin."

Roger gaped at him. "No way!"

"I was."

Alex was no longer smiling. "I guess I wasn't paying attention. What's Aberlin?"

Roger began, "It was this town in—" He looked at Sean. "Sorry."

"Go ahead," Sean told him. "It's in the past now."

In a lower voice, Roger said, "Aberlin was a small town in Scotland. It had about the same number of people in it as Marsport, I think. Anyway, the Levelers hit it with a biobomb about ten, eleven years ago. They were calling for everyone not of British descent to leave the islands. Load of rubbish, but they said that if they didn't get their way, they'd destroy one town a month. Almost everyone in Aberlin died of a modified form of plague. Sean was one of the few survivors. You were raised in the States, right?"

"Yeah."

"Which explains why you don't sound Scottish.

But they caught that ring of terrorists. They're all in prison now."

"Yeah," Sean said bitterly. "And my parents are still dead."

Patrick put a hand on Sean's shoulder. "This is a new world," he said. "A new beginning."

Sean turned in a few minutes later. With his door closed, he couldn't even hear the others. He knew they'd be talking about him, though—the only Asimov Project kid to come in on this flight, and the last one scheduled to come to Mars. They might even be feeling sorry for him.

The bed felt strange at first. During the whole flight out from Earth, for many months, Sean had slept in a pressure web, a zero-gravity sleeping bag made up of elastic tubing that alternately inflated and deflated, the kneading massage keeping his muscles toned and his circulation healthy.

But he had slept in worse places. He could remember nights in burned-out cars, shivering nights in the scant shelter of a couple of loose boards, nights on pavement, on mounds of garbage, in downpours.

Well, now at least he had his own room, even if it was gray and exactly like every other bedroom on the entire planet. And he had friends.

If he could trust them.

Sean drifted to sleep, and for some reason he dreamed of his first foster family. They had invited media reporters to interview Sean. He had learned later that they charged for the interviews. The two of them hadn't been a very happy couple, though when the cameras were on them, they were smiling and looked cheerful.

But every night Sean had gone to bed listening to them screaming at each other. And every morning he had dreaded getting up to their complaints and sometimes their blows. Both of them were quick to hit if he put a toe out of line.

Now, in his dreams, he heard them screaming:

"We could have held up United News for twice what you got!"

"You moron! Who'd pay that much to broadcast the brat saying he doesn't remember the attack? It's old news now!"

With a gasp, Sean sat up in the dark, nearly tumbling out of bed. At first he felt confused, his head reeling. Then it came back to him: Gravity was different here. It was a different world, a new start. It was Mars.

Marsport was a grand experiment. Earth was overcrowded, bickering, on the verge of breakdown. If a new world could be opened, then the people of Earth would have hope for the future. It had taken years of work to build and equip the colony. Now the goal was for it to exist without any kind of resupply from Earth. It had to do that for at least one full Martian year before it would be considered a success. Then, once the colonists had proved that it could be done, others would come from Earth to make Mars a planet where humans could live permanently. But that all hinged on the population of Marsport surviving for one full Martian year with absolutely no food or equipment coming from Earth in that time. If everything went right, the experiment in survival would begin in just a few months.

Sean settled down again, pulling the blanket back over himself.

Survival.

He was pretty good at that.

CHAPTER 3

Mondays, Wednesdays, and Fridays were English, mathematics, history, and physical education. Tuesdays and Thursdays were science, computers, and social studies. The twenty young colonists of the Asimov Project had classes from eight o'clock to two, and then they were expected to participate in the work of the colony.

Sean settled into the routine easily enough. Although all twenty students met in the same education dome, their lessons were all different, all delivered by computer. Sean got to know the others, and he liked some of them a lot. Alex had somehow become his best friend, but Jenny Laslo was a close second. Nickie Mikhailova, who was sixteen, was Jenny's best friend. She reminded Sean a little of Ellman—like him, she was stocky and square of build. "That's what comes from having a long line of Russian peasants as ancestors," she joked. But her face, framed by short strawberry-blond hair, was always impish and pleasant, and her knowledge of computers was second to none.

And then there was Elizabeth Ling. She was the same age as Alex—fourteen and a half—and had the longest hair of anyone Sean had met in the colony. It was jet black and hung down to her shoulders. She was very quiet, very pale, and very solemn. She never laughed, and Sean secretly sympathized with her. He didn't laugh much himself.

In the classes, Sean felt as if he were the stupidest person on the planet. The others had specialties already. He didn't. The others raced through problems that he had to sit and stare at. Sean began to wonder if he were just a charity case—if Amanda had arranged for him to come to Mars out of pity. He tried not to show how inferior he felt around Jenny and Elizabeth, though. Sometimes that was hard to do, especially when Jenny went into lecture mode and began to point out things he had no way of knowing. At times like those, Sean put on an expression of bored impatience, as if he didn't need the information, and that only made him feel worse—a phony in more ways than one.

3.2

At the end of his first week in the colony, Jenny dropped by after breakfast. "Want to go outside?"

Sean, who had nothing to look forward to other than trying to catch up on math homework, asked, "Can we do that?"

"Just got permission from Ellman," replied Jenny with a grin. "He's okay if you know how to talk to him. You've trained in a pressure suit, right?"

"On Luna," Sean said. "I passed my level one tests."

"Ice!" Jenny said. "There's a catch, though. We

have to go out in groups of three or more, so we'll need someone else. Where's Alex?"

They found him in one of the greenhouses, where he was reading a disk on piloting. He scrambled up from where he had been sitting in the shade of some tall cornstalks, looking embarrassed. "Nobody ever comes here on Saturday," he said. "That's why I like to study here. Nice and quiet."

Sean understood that, but he also understood that the greenhouse, with its lush aroma of growing things, its supplemental lights that imitated the sun as it shone on Earth, and its warm, moist air was one place that felt like home.

"Want to go out?" Jenny asked. "Not for long, but just to show Sean the sights?"

"Such as they are," Alex said with a chuckle. "Okay, I'm in."

The three of them made their way to an entry dome, where they donned the clumsy pressure suits, then waited in an airlock as pumps sucked the air out. Sean's heart was beating fast with excitement, and every time he took a breath the air rattled in his helmet, sounding like pebbles falling down a chute. Finally the outer door opened, and Alex led the way out.

It was cold. At this latitude the maximum outside temperature at noon in summer could get up to fifteen degrees Celsius—not quite sixty degrees on the old Fahrenheit scale. It was barely spring, though, and on this particular Saturday noon, the thermometer would have read minus six Celsius, well below freezing. Alex's voice rasped over the radio receiver in Sean's helmet: "We can't stay out very long in unheated suits."

"Why didn't we use heated ones?" Sean asked.

"Because we're not part of a work party, and they're reserved. Hey, Jenn, let's go look at the construction site where they're sinking the new thermal well."

Walking was difficult. The ground underfoot was loose sand scattered with boulders of all sizes. The sun hung overhead, pale and shrunken in the dark blue sky. The three of them rounded the edge of the dome, and Sean caught his breath.

The day was clear, and the towering, rugged cliffs at the base of Olympus Mons looked close enough to touch. They were almost sheer, and they reared up four miles above the foothills. Beyond them was the bulk of Olympus itself, so large that it looked as if the horizon was warped upward, vanishing in a dim purple distance. On the foothills past the settlement a forest of windmills rose, hundreds of them, their great blades sweeping in a gentle breeze.

Jenny pointed, and her voice crackled on the radio, "In the spring we'll have real storms, and the generators will have to be cleaned about every other day. They're sealed against dust, but it gets in everywhere during the seasonal storms. The windmills are shut down during the peak winds, but we'll be out a lot then. That's one of our jobs, keeping the generators working."

Sean felt a vibration through the soles of his feet,

and a second later he heard a dull boom that did not come over the radio. "What was that?"

"Blasting," Alex said. "The air's so thin that it doesn't make half the noise it would on Earth. There, see? No, look over to the left. They're drilling a shaft right down into the crust. There's still volcanic heat deep down, and that powers turbine generators."

Sean was shivering from the cold. They could see a work crew in the distance, six figures in bright blue pressure suits under a billowing plume of dust from the explosion.

"This is close enough," Jenny said. "Let's get back inside. I'm freezing!" She turned, the sun gleaming on her helmet.

They retraced their steps and went back inside. Sean felt himself gasping. "Seems hard to breathe," he complained.

Alex hung up his pressure suit. "That's because you were on a richer oxygen mix outside. In here it's lower than Earth's normal, a mix of oxygen, argon, helium, and nitrogen. But the tanks give you full oxygen, because usually when you're outside you're doing manual labor."

"All the oxygen comes from Mars?" Sean asked. He knew that on Earth's moon oxygen came from factories that broke down oxygen-containing minerals.

"Pretty much," Jenny said. "The greenhouse plants generate a tiny fraction of what we're breathing, but most of it comes from the regolith, the basic rock of Mars. A lot of the minerals that make up the rock are oxides, and one thing the colonists have to do is to build a chain of solar-powered oxygen factories all around the planet. Now that the air's thicker, we have to make sure that eventually we can breathe it."

"Some of the oxygen comes from water, too," Alex added. "There are underground, automated factories near the south pole that will mine subsurface ice and then break it into hydrogen and oxygen. When the factories are fully operational, the gases will be piped back here."

Sean was beginning to feel warm again. They headed back to what was generally called the town hall, a community structure where meetings could be held, games could be played, and meals could be eaten. It had been one of the first habitats for humans on Mars, and years ago it had suffered a blowout when the shell burst and the air had exploded outward. Colonists had repaired and reinforced it with a cage of tubular steel, made right on Mars. The hall itself was proof that the colonists wouldn't give up easily and would bounce back from disaster, or so Sean had been told in his orientation sessions.

Weekends were a time of relaxation, though work never completely stopped in the colony. They found the hall about half full of colonists, some of the younger ones tossing a ball around, others deep in discussion at tables along the walls, and still others eating. Sean, Alex, and Jenny joined this last group.

Alex made a face as he checked the menu. "Great. Tuna salad or vegetarian today. Yuck."

"One day we'll be eating only food we produce

ourselves," Jenny said. "Right now about half is reconstituted stuff from Earth. Think of it as survival rations."

"I'd give a lot for a pizza," complained Alex.

"Hi, guys." Mickey Goldberg breezed over and pulled up a seat at their table. "What are you three up to?"

Sean told him about their brief stroll out in the open. Mickey chuckled. "You know why we have those unheated suits? It's to keep us from roaming around too far from safety. Hey, Jenny, tell them about the time you nearly froze!"

Jenny's face turned red. "I didn't nearly freeze. I just stayed out too long."

"Uh-huh," Mickey said in a teasing voice. "Just long enough for the emergency sensor to sound. Simak had to send out a rescue party to bring you back in."

"I walked back in on my own, didn't I?" demanded Jenny. "I didn't even have frostbite."

Mickey laughed. "Well, Sean, just wait until

they want you to do some work. Then you'll get one of the fancy blue suits. They're heated, and have auxiliary boosters built in, so you can lift half a ton. You feel like some kind of cartoon hero in one of those things. Hey, have you been assigned a specialty yet?"

Sean looked down at his plate of half-eaten tuna salad. "Not yet."

"Give him time," Jenny said. "He just got here."

Mickey shrugged. "Okay, okay. I just thought he might have decided to be a survival specialist or something. I mean, he's famous for having survived back on Earth, right?"

"Let him alone, Mickey," Alex said. "Sean will be fine."

"Everyone's touchy today," Mickey said, getting up. "Okay, I'm going. See you guys around." Mickey bounced away, looking like a kangaroo.

A moment later, Ellman's voice lashed out: "Goldberg! Walk properly when you're not in a gymnasium."

"Good," Sean said. "He had it coming."

"Don't let him get to you," Jenny said. "He's too energetic for his own good, and sometimes his mouth is a few steps ahead of his brain, you know?"

After a few moments of silence, Alex asked, "So what was it like, back on Earth, when you were running with the gang?"

Sean shrugged. "I did what I had to do to live, that's all. I don't want to talk about it."

Alex leaned back in his chair. "I was just curious—"

Sean jumped up. "I don't want to talk about it, okay?" He snatched up his tray, but he had momentarily forgotten the low gravity. The tray catapulted the remains of his tuna salad, and it flew over his head. A second later, a hand clamped on his shoulder, and he turned to face a scarlet-faced Dr. Ellman. A blotch of tuna salad spattered the front of his tunic. "We do not have food fights in Marsport, Doe," he growled. "No matter how barbaric your upbringing was, you will have some manners here.

Confined to quarters until Monday!"

Sean didn't even try to apologize. He slunk off to his room, feeling more out of place than ever.

Sean wasn't really bothered that his room was tiny, but he was aware of how impersonal it looked. The others had been here longer and their rooms seemed more lived-in. Alex had models of airplanes and spacecraft hanging from his ceiling, and posters of pilots and zooming ships on his walls. Roger had papered his walls with photos of his parents and holographic posters of ancient sites on Earth—the Pyramids of Egypt, the great stone heads of Easter Island, and a dozen others.

Sean spent the weekend in his bare room or the common area, glumly reviewing his academic assignments and watching an old movie or two on his console. Once he caught part of a news broadcast from Earth, a tightly beamed narrowcast sent directly to Mars. There was nothing very encouraging: Leveler riots in Australia and South America, a serious crop failure in Central Asia, border wars in half a dozen places. It should have made Sean glad to be on Mars, but in his current mood, nothing could have done that.

Monday brought release from his captivity, but not from his sour mood. One thing he had noticed from the beginning: People were eager to talk to him. Marsport got very little news directly from Earth, and new arrivals could expect to be pumped for the latest information. Sean told them what he could. Earth was suffering from ecological disasters, war, and riots. Levelers were waging a kind of guerrilla campaign against the richest nations, using sabotage, kidnapping, and even murder to present their list of demands.

Dr. Ellman stopped Sean in a corridor one afternoon and said, "A word to the wise, Doe. You have your own opinions about conditions on Earth. Those are colored by your, ah, peculiar history."

The heavyset man made a face, as if Sean's history were Sean's own fault. "That's no reason to go around upsetting everyone with your tales of how civilization is about to collapse."

Sean's anger boiled up in him. "They asked me!" he said. "And things are getting worse. Unless—"

"I don't want to hear it," Ellman said. "If you're a disruptive element in the colony, Doe, you can be sent back to Earth when the transport leaves. It's your choice." Ellman turned and stalked away.

That week other distractions arrived. The *Argosy* was still in orbit, and the landers began to ferry supplies from Earth down to the surface. That meant a slightly varied choice of foods, and the colonists perked up at the prospect of changing what had become a monotonous diet.

But classes were hard as ever. Sean struggled, strained, and became quieter and quieter. And he felt more inadequate than he ever had before in his life.

Not even Jenny's friendship could lift his mood. She was smart—no, she was *brilliant*. Sean was in awe of how fast she picked up everything. The toughest equation was as simple as the alphabet to her, and she seemed to have a photographic memory for names, dates, and places. Once or twice she complained that the educational programs were wrong or misleading, and when Tim Mpondo, who was supervising the education of the Asimov Project kids, challenged her, she was able to produce research that proved her point. Ellman, Sean thought, would have exploded over something like that, but Mpondo just said, "Interesting. Well, I'll reprogram the questions, then. Good work, Laslo."

His own studies were a steady grind. Sean liked reading, and he did well enough in writing and literature, but the math was extremely difficult and the science all but impossible. Time after time he caused explosions in his chemistry lab. Fortunately, it was a virtual lab, computer-generated, so he didn't actually cause any damage, but it was discouraging to hear Mickey Goldberg sing out, "Heads down, everybody—Doe's got his hands on a test tube again!"

And Mickey seemed to have made it his mission in life to pester Sean about his specialty. He asked the same question about four or five times a week: "What are you going to settle in and actually do, Sean? Haven't they placed you yet?" Sometimes he had suggestions: "You could go in for demolition. You have a real talent at blowing things up!" Or: "You know, if you went outside at night and stuck your arms straight out, you'd freeze solid. You might make a good coat rack."

Sean, who had fought off boys older and tougher than Mickey back on Earth, held back his temper and merely simmered. He still could not explain it, and he supposed it might have just been stress, but increasingly Sean had the feeling that matters back on Earth were becoming more serious. Whatever happened, he did not want to be bundled back aboard the *Argosy* when it departed for Earth in three months.

He had the sick feeling it might be flying back for Doomsday.

4.1

"What about the crop failures?" Jenny asked, her brow furrowed.

"Lots of them," Sean replied, huffing. He, Jenny, and eight other kids were taking their turn in the gym. In the low gravity of Mars, it was essential for the colonists to work to maintain their muscle tone, and that meant five hours of hard exercise a week. Sean and Jenny were side by side on treadmills, running with the strange low stride necessary on Mars. She was faster than he was, and she wasn't even gasping. "Central Asia lost half its rice harvest two years ago—plant viruses left over from the China-Russia war. And some of the rainforest in south Asia is infected."

Jenny leaned forward, grasping the safety handles

of her treadmill and making it whir even louder. Sean realized she was angry.

"What about countermeasures? Bioengineering?"

"Expensive," Sean gasped. He was used to being grilled about conditions on Earth. Some of the colonists, the old hands, had been on Mars for five years now. Dr. Ellman had been the science and communications officer for the first ten-person crew to erect a habitat on Mars, and others had been on the planet nearly as long. Though they received news reports from home every day, they still burned with curiosity.

"Stupid, stupid," Jenny was growling. "How can it be too expensive? If the ecology crashes, there'll be worldwide disease, starvation—too expensive!" Her treadmill chimed, telling her that she had finished her three-mile run. She began to slow her pace, the treadmill automatically adapting as Jenny cooled down.

Sean couldn't answer. His lungs were burning, and sweat poured into his eyes. He'd heard of the runner's second wind, but he couldn't seem to find his. He told himself he wouldn't look at the readout, then gave in and glanced down. The display read 4.7 kilometers—just a little left to do. He clenched his teeth and tried to increase speed. No good. He was running full-tilt already.

A moment later, thankfully, he heard the chime of his own readout. He'd done his 4.8 kilometers— three miles. Like Jenny, he began to slow until he was shuffling along in a sliding walk. He slowed to a stop, stepped off the treadmill, and reached for a towel.

Jenny had looped her towel around her neck. She held both ends of it as Sean wiped his face. "I heard that some large animal species have gone extinct," she said.

Sean groaned. "Let me get my breath, or *I'll* go extinct," he panted. A few moments later he said, "Elephants are extinct in the wild now. And gorillas. They survive in artificial habitats, though."

"What about—"

"Jenny, please. I'll tell you everything I know, really. But I've got to take a shower!"

It was, as always, a brief one. Marsport recycled everything, including its water, but even so, 3,212 colonists used a lot of water. Inevitably, some of it escaped. Sean had learned that the easily mined permafrost deposits were just about exhausted. The colony was planning construction on a pipeline to bring water in from the south polar region, but that project was still in the future. At present, colonists had a ration of four showers per week, with a two-and-a-half-minute maximum. That meant you soaped and rinsed fast. It also meant that most colonists kept their hair cut short—shampoos took even more water, and the colony just couldn't afford it. Lake Ares, the emergency reservoir, might be tapped, true, but Jenny reacted to that suggestion with horror. There were *fish* in there! It was a biological *habitat!*

And it was a last-ditch reservoir, if everything else failed. Sean knew that and understood it, even if he resented the beep that told him he had twenty seconds to rinse off any remaining soap.

He dried, dressed, and met Jenny in the gym again.

"Want to get a snack or something?" she asked.

"Sure," he agreed. School had ended for the day, and they had nothing in particular to do for a couple of hours. They went to a general mess dome with fifteen small tables and eight or nine other diners. Now that the *Argosy* had unloaded, they enjoyed a wider selection of meals, including some actual freeze-dried meats. Jenny, who was trying hard to be a vegetarian, had a kind of vegetable stew. Sean chose a hamburger, though it was made with soy protein.

"How much of the food is from the greenhouses?" he asked as they settled in at one of the tables.

"More than half," Jenny said. "In fact, the colony could probably survive just with the greenhouse food. It'd be kind of dull, though. Lots of algae-based protein!"

Sean made a face. He'd tried algae-based protein. It was faintly green, clumpy, and bland, with a flavor reminiscent of, well, algae. "Yuck."

"You can develop a taste for it." Jenny ate some of her stew. "But I have to admit, it's great to get freeze-dried veggies from home now and then. We just don't have the variety yet."

Sean munched his burger. It wasn't great, but he'd eaten worse, like roasted rat and pigeon.

"I guess the *Argosy* is about ready to go back to Earth," he said.

"Another two months, I think," Jenny told him. "There are some mineral samples and some seismic readouts the scientists on Earth want to get their hands on. The series won't be complete until then. They'll be cutting it close. There aren't that many times a year when a ship can launch from Martian orbit on a good return trajectory to Earth. They'll *have* to take off in about twelve weeks, or else wait another six months."

When they had finished eating, they went to an observation dome to look out at the Martian surface. Sean had arrived at the very beginning of spring in this hemisphere. The changes the season brought were extreme. Sandstorms whipped across the surface now, fierce gales filled with fine, gritty dust that sandblasted everything exposed on the surface. The heating—if you could call it that—also raised dust devils. Now that the surface reached a balmy ten degrees Celsius—about fifty Fahrenheit—at noon, the storms regularly rose up.

They were spectacular, tornadoes of whirling dust towering more than a mile high, leaning, racing across the Martian surface. As Jenny and Sean looked out to the south where there were few buildings, they saw three of the dust devils snaking their way toward the colony. "They're more danger-ous than the sandstorms," Jenny said. "Lucky they're small. The winds get to tremendous speeds."

The storms dangled and twirled like ropes, vanish-ing into a clear sky. Unlike Earth tornadoes, they rose from the surface. The three gigantic whirlwinds did an intricate dance, weaving in and out of each other's paths. Sean winced as one of them swept over a dis-tant dome. "Could they break open an installation?"

"They haven't so far," Jenny said. "I think the domes are safe—they're engineered to resist high wind velocities. Some of the red-coded connecting tubes are iffy. We're not supposed to go into them if there are storms in the area. But if a tube cracked, the doors at both ends would seal automatically."

"What if someone was inside?"

"Too bad," Jenny said.

Sean shivered.

4.2

Two days later Sean learned about the kind of damage a dust devil could do. It happened during his chemistry session, which was overseen by a glowering Dr. Ellman. Sean, Mickey Goldberg, Alex Benford, Patrick Nakoma, and Nickie Mikhailova were all at separate virtual stations, each working on an individual problem, when everything went haywire.

The three-dimensional display in front of Sean flickered, flared, and faded out. The other students yelped in dismay as they lost their work too. Nickie, who was a computer-science specialist, said, "We lost core power! What happened?"

Ellman, who had been watching Alex's virtual titration experiment, snarled, "I don't know, unless Doe somehow managed to destroy the circuitry. I suppose you're innocent, Doe?"

"I didn't do anything!" Sean protested.

Ellman looked at him with a sour sneer. "You never do, and that's one of your problems!" The lights in the lab dimmed suddenly, leaving them in semidarkness. "Go to your quarters. We'll take up here next session. I trust we will have power again then."

But when they headed back to their dormitory wing, Alex, in the lead, found that the yellow-coded door to the connecting tube was sealed and wouldn't open. "Man, I wonder what's up. Let's go up to the observation dome and see."

They wound their way up the stairs to the top of the lab dome, where windows looked out over the colony. A noise that Sean had barely been aware of, a sort of grinding, grew as they climbed, and when they got to the top he saw that the whole south side of the dome was being assaulted by dust whipping against the windows, driven by a roaring wind. It lasted for just a few seconds, and then the dust screeched overhead and the storm swept on. "Look at that!" Alex exclaimed.

Sean pressed his face against a clear window. Dozens of dust devils were writhing through the colony, and in the distance, up in the foothills, more were snaking through the forests of windmills.

"That's it," Mickey said. "The wind generators have shut down."

"Some of them are damaged," Nickie said, shading her eyes with both hands. "They'll have to be repaired."

"I'm volunteering," Patrick said at once.

"Not me," Mickey said flatly. "I don't want to

be caught out in the open when a storm hits."

"I'll go," Sean said.

Mickey glanced at him and grinned. "Oh, so you've discovered your specialty at last. Going to become a planetary hero, are you?"

"Stop it, Goldberg," Nickie said. "Somebody has to go out and clean the contacts, and it might as well be us. We can't get back to school until the colony has full power. You know our computers are the first things to go when there's a power shortage."

"I could use a week or two off," Mickey said. "Might be a good idea to let old Sean go out on the repair mission. Think you can foul things up just enough to keep us out of school, Doe?"

"Shut up," Sean said irritably. "I don't care if you don't want to go outside, but I'm tired of being cooped up. If I can be useful, I'm going, that's all."

Mickey laughed. "That's the pioneering spirit. Just like you, too. You were in the news a lot back on Earth, right? I'll bet you miss not having your face on broadcasts every day. Must be pretty dull for you up here on Mars. Hey, I've got it. Your specialty can be 'Celebrity First-Class.'"

"Mickey," said Patrick in a warning tone. "Enough."

"Okay, okay," Mickey said. "Just kidding, Sean. You go out there and do your best."

When they went downstairs again, they found a repair crew at work. Two men had taken up a section of the flooring in front of the closed tube door, revealing a meter-wide, meter-deep trench lined with pipes and conduits. "Air leak in the tube?" Mickey asked.

One of the men glanced up as the other slid down into the trench on his back. "No, but the power loss caused the emergency locks to engage. We'll go in and clear it. Meanwhile, you guys can get back to your quarters by going through town hall and the west greenhouse wing."

Sean and the others found their way back to the dorms by the alternate route, a long and winding one that left Sean half lost. Patrick talked with the captain of the repair crew, a woman named Sandy Colmer, and reported that she was delighted to take volunteers. "Come on," he said. "We've got to go to a training session, or she won't take us."

That led them to one of the outlying domes—one crowded with surface transport rovers, spare parts, and what looked like stacks of junk. Patrick called the rovers "Martian limos," but to Sean they looked like stripped-down Army tanks. Sandy Colmer, a tall, black-haired woman of thirty, assembled her team there.

Sean counted eighteen people in all, quite a crowd for the area. Alex was easily the youngest, with Sean and Patrick next. The only other student volunteer was Leslie Kristopolis, a botany specialist Sean did not know well. He thought she was about seventeen, a slender girl with short, curly red hair. She saw the others and came over to stand with them. "I haven't been outside for months," she said by way of greeting. "I'm about to get cabin fever."

Patrick shushed her. At the front of the gathering

Sandy was holding up a generator nacelle, the unit at the top of the windmills. "This is the problem," she was saying. "The dust gets into the bearings around this axle. What we have to do is take each one apart, replace the bearing assembly, and then reattach the vanes. The hard part will be the climbing. The weight isn't a problem. Now, to detach the bearing assembly, you have to remove these restraining rings and then loosen these six bolts—"

They watched, and then each of them had to disassemble and reassemble the unit. It took hours, with Sandy criticizing their technique and offering suggestions. "When do we go?" Patrick asked.

"Not tonight," Sandy told him. "Too cold and too dark. We'll start just after sunrise tomorrow. We have about fifty units out of commission. That's too many for one day, so we'll work on about ten at a time. Plan for four mornings."

"Why not—," began Sean, but then he stopped short.

"Why not work all day?" Sandy asked with a grin.

Sean nodded. "But I already know the answer. We might get caught outside when the dust storms come in the afternoon."

"Right," Sandy said. "And believe me, you don't want that to happen. It's dangerous enough out there as it is."

4.3

"You what?!" yelped Jenny.

"I volunteered to help repair the windmills," Sean said irritably. "That's all. I didn't set fire to Dr. Ellman or anything."

"That's crazy!" Jenny said. "You don't know anything about electronics."

They were sitting in the dimmed-out common area. Patrick Nakoma said, "Relax, Jenny. There's not that much to know. The dust gets in the bearings, you switch out the bearings. Bring the fouled ones in for cleaning, leave fresh ones in their place. It's not that hard."

"But you have to climb up the towers!" Jenny made an impatient gesture. "They're a hundred meters high! The vanes are fifty meters long! Anything could happen out there!"

"We'll have safety harnesses," Patrick said. "Really, it's no big deal. And we'll watch out for each other. Nothing's going to go wrong."

"What if a storm sweeps up while you're at the top of one of those towers?" Jenny demanded. "If dust tears your suit, you could die of oxygen starvation or freeze to death! This is crazy."

"I want to do it," Sean said. "Look, I can't just spend my time here going to lessons and running on treadmills. I'm not contributing anything. Mickey's right—I've got no specialty, I'm dead weight. This isn't much, but it's something I can do for the colony. And anyway, I'd rather do this than have Ellman leaning over my shoulder telling me how stupid I am!"

"But going out when—"

"You went out and got yourself lost once," Sean pointed out. "Mickey Goldberg said—"

Jenny stiffened. "Mickey was wrong. I didn't get lost. I just lost track of the time, that's all. And anyway, that was completely different!"

"I'm going tomorrow," Sean said. "That's settled."

Jenny got to her feet. "Boys can be so stupid!" She hurried out, her back stiff.

"And girls are always so reasonable," Patrick said with a chuckle after she had gone. "Don't worry, Sean. I won't say a repair crew isn't dangerous, but we'll be looking out for each other. Better get some sleep. We'll have a hard day tomorrow."

The blue pressure suit was more confining than it looked. Sean had struggled into it—a three-layered suit, heated, with supplemental oxygen and a full helmet. He flexed his hands inside protective gloves. He had worn them to practice the repairs, but he still wondered how well he would be able to handle the tools when he was perched up on one of the towers. Sandy gave the word and all eighteen of the repair crew clambered into three surface rovers, six to a vehicle. Sean, Alex, Patrick, and Leslie were all in the last one to rumble out of the dome.

The shrunken sun was up, low on the horizon, and pale shadows stretched out across the rusty red Martian landscape. The rovers traveled abreast because each one kicked up a cloud of dust from its treads. If they had gone single file, the last two in line would be traveling blind.

Sean knew they weren't really going all that fast, but to him it seemed they were racing across the surface, swerving around large boulders and outcrops, then following a rough road that twisted up into the foothills. The towers of the windmills seemed to grow as they approached, larger and larger, tall open-meshed structures of steel and alloy polished to a gleaming finish by the punishing dust. It looked as if every third or fourth windmill was frozen, its vanes not moving at all. A half-dozen or so were already damaged, the vanes bent and twisted by the cruel dust devils.

Patrick pointed at one of the twisted windmills and said, "We'll just remove the vanes from those and leave them for the pros to fix." His voice came crackling into Sean's helmet, sounding distant and scratchy.

Sean fiddled with the controls on his suit belt. The heat had been welcome at first, but he had overdone it. Now he was starting to smell his own sweat. He knew he would be in for an uncomfortable six hours if he couldn't get the suit's heater adjusted.

The first rover stopped at the base of one of the

windmills, and a two-person team leaped out. Looking back, Sean saw them scrambling up the access ladder looking like spiders swarming up a web. The windmill was nearly a thousand feet tall— over three hundred meters. His stomach lurched. How would he handle a height like that?

"Patrick," Leslie said, "will you partner me?"

"You've got it," Patrick replied. "Alex, you and Sean will be okay with each other, won't you?"

"Sure," Alex said, his voice tense.

Sean realized he wasn't the only one on edge.

Another stop, then another, and the first rover turned to make its way back to the first windmill to wait for that team. More stops, until the six people in Sean's transport began to climb out two at a time.

And at last only he and Alex were left. The transport rumbled to a halt. The windmill towered up and up, its vanes twisted and bent. They had drawn one of the really bad ones.

"Okay," Alex said, getting up. "All we have to do

is take off the vanes, lower them down, and then climb down ourselves. Piece of cake, right?"

"Sure," Sean said, trying to sound more confident than he felt.

But as he looked at the ladder that led up into the Martian sky for more than the length of a football field, he felt a pang of doubt.

What if Jenny was right?

CHAPTER 5

You climbed until your arms ached, and then you hung there in the open, resting, unable to wipe away the sweat that stung your eyes. Ahead of you, a long way off, were the fantastic cliffs at the foot of Olympus Mons, so high that you couldn't see over them to the vast bulk of the mountain. On either side of you the foothills rolled away to an abrupt horizon. The blue sky was etched with high, thin clouds, like frost on a windowpane back on Earth. But you weren't here to admire the landscape, so you forced your aching arms and legs to drag you higher, step by step, up the endless ladder.

Sean clenched his teeth, trying not to think about how far he'd come, how much of a drop lay beneath him already. He didn't look down, but up.

And yet the windmill nacelle didn't seem to come any closer. Sean told himself that the climb wasn't as hard as it looked. After all, he didn't weigh half as much on Mars as he had on Earth. Still, his senses told him that he was already unreasonably high on a rickety structure, and he had the panicky feeling that one wrong step would plunge him to his death.

Of course, there was the safety line, a tether that snicked into a track in the ladder handrail. A sudden downward pull would make it act like a brake, slowing and stopping any fall. But the line seemed absurdly thin to hold him.

Sean forced himself to stop thinking and start climbing again—he had paused momentarily—and he looked up. "You keeping up okay?" he asked his partner, his voice strained.

"Fine," said Alex with a grunt. Alex was below him on the ladder, doggedly making his way up with a long line coiled at his belt.

Up and up, and finally the top of the structure did

begin to grow near as the tower became narrower. The last ten feet were the hardest, because by that time the tower seemed so thin and insubstantial. It did nothing to hide the view, or the fact that Sean was now hundreds of feet above the surface. At the top Sean stepped out onto a narrow circular catwalk, held the rail tight with one hand, and used the other hand to unclip his safety line from the rail. He reclipped it into a track just below the nacelle.

Alex joined him, looked around. "What a view!"

Sean could feel his heart beating hard. "Let's get this done."

But he could see the view too: The dull morning sun gleamed off Marsport, a spread-out network of metal and glass domes and connecting corridors. The roadway beneath them showed the ruts left by the transports. Swirling across the plain and through Marsport were other tracks: the skittery paths of dust devils, some only a few feet across, a few monstrous ones a kilometer or more.

Alex was on the other side of the nacelle now.

"Clipped in?" Sean asked. "Double check."

Alex tugged his safety line, and Sean retested his. "Okay, let's hook up."

Alex fastened a small pulley to the support rail just below the nacelle. He threaded line through it, letting the coil fall and leaving a few meters free. The nose cone of the windmill blades unscrewed in a clockwise direction, opposite to most fasteners. The rotor axle had been frozen in place by dust, so Sean had no trouble removing the cone. He dropped it, as Sandy had instructed them to do, but did not watch its fall to the surface.

"Okay," Sean said. "Clip the line to the hoist ring."

The hoist ring was normally hidden by the nose cone. Alex clipped the line to it and said, "Secure."

"Check the brake."

"It's okay."

Sean reached to his belt and took out a wrench. He used it to loosen and remove six bolts that held the blades onto the axle. When he had put the bolts into his belt pouch, he and Alex jiggled and pushed until the blades came free. The line and pulley held them.

"Let me get around and we'll lower away."

Alex moved back around the circular catwalk, and Sean ducked under the line. He released the brake on the pulley—not completely, but enough to let the windmill blades sink down. Alex, his leg braced around one of the tower struts, let the line out gradually. If the pulley failed, it would be up to Alex to let the assembly down slowly, preventing a damaging fall.

The line was almost at an end when Sean, holding tight and looking almost straight down, said, "Okay, that's good. Let the line fall and I'll get the pulley." He felt dizzy, with the strange sensation that the whole tower was tilting, and he looked away from the distant ground with a sense of relief. He tugged the remainder of the line through the pulley and let it fall. Then he unclipped the pulley. "One down."

"Here comes our ride."

Gripping the rail as if his life depended on it, Sean looked down again. He could see the dust of the approaching transport. "Let's go."

And then the long climb down, almost as much of a strain as the climb up. When they reached the ground, they found the transport had passed them by. Alex took the line from the blade assembly and recoiled it. The line was deceptively thin, but more than three hundred meters long, and it made a heavy-looking coil. "Guess we were too slow."

"Sandy wants to get as many of these done today as she can," Sean said. "They'll be back for us."

He didn't add that he, for one, was glad for the delay. His aching shoulders and knees needed the rest.

He and Alex managed three repairs that first day. Sean felt a sense of satisfaction after the second windmill, when they simply had to replace the dust-jammed bearings. As soon as they had reached the ground after that one, they had looked up. The huge vanes were sweeping around, responding to a breeze so gentle that Sean wasn't even aware of it. But each turn of the blades meant that the colony had a little more electricity. At last, Sean thought, he was doing something.

The first day's work ended, and the transports hurried them back to Marsport. "Could've done more," Leslie grumbled. "No dust devils today. Too cloudy."

That was true enough. The hazy clouds of the morning had given way to a high, dense, gray overcast. Without the sun's heat to raise them, the dust devils wouldn't be dancing. Still, Sean was grateful that the day's work was done. He was too sore and stiff to even think about climbing another windmill.

The others wanted to talk about their day, but Jenny didn't want to hear any of it. Sean felt irritated with her. She had been the first person on Mars to show him any kind of friendship. What had gone wrong? Now she seemed to think he was being some kind of show-off for volunteering. He caught up with her in the common room that evening before lights out, but even then she didn't want to talk.

"Look," Sean told her, "it isn't hard. Anybody could do what Alex and I are doing. And it does help the colony. By the time we're finished, we'll have full power again."

"We could have full power if they'd finish the stupid thermal turbos," Jenny snapped. "They're buried in the ground beneath Olympus Mons. They wouldn't fail every time there was a dust storm!"

Sean had learned about the thermal generators. Even though Olympus Mons had not erupted in millions of years, it still had heat deep inside it. The thermal generators would eventually be planted deep in the heart of the old volcano, where subsurface heat would be used to generate electricity for the colony. One was already in place and working, but drilling and putting them in place was a difficult, involved process. It would be years before enough turbo generators to supply all the colony's needs were in place.

"Somebody's got to repair the windmills," Sean said. "And I'm glad to do it. I want to be more than just a body who takes up space."

"Because Mickey Goldberg keeps teasing you!"

"I'm not doing this because of Mickey!"

Jenny gave him an exasperated look. "Marsport has too many specialists already! We need some . . . some generalists, too! Sean, you've been through so much on Earth that . . . well, I mean, you don't have anything to prove."

"Mars isn't Earth," Sean said simply.

She glared at him. "No, but boys are always boys, aren't they? Okay, play your macho games if you want to, but if you break your neck out there, don't expect me to be upset!" And again she jumped up and hurried out.

That night Sean felt as if he were nothing more than a collection of aches and pains. He tossed and turned in his bunk, trying without success to find a position that would let him rest more easily. It took him ages to fall asleep, and when he did he fell into a repeated dream of climbing ladders. He could feel the pressure of the rungs under his feet, could feel the rails in his hands. But the dream ladder led up and up into oblivion, stretching so far into the deep sky of Mars that it vanished. And although he didn't dare look down, Sean knew that beneath him, step by step, the ladder was dissolving, vanishing.

If he wanted to live, he would have to climb forever.

5.3

Morning came before he was ready for it. Sean climbed out of bed feeling groggy, his muscles still stiff. His pressure suit had been cleaned, but he imagined that it still stank of sweat. This morning the repair crews didn't engage in much banter. A fourth rover joined them, this one hauling a long, long trailer with windmill blades stacked in it. The lead transport's crew would be replacing vanes this morning. The other two would work on bearings and on taking down other bent blades.

Leslie groaned as the transport jounced and rattled. "I've got aches that have aches of their own," she complained.

Patrick nudged her boot with his. "You're just out of shape, Les. You've gotten too used to puttering around with algae tanks. Do you good to get outside and get a little fresh Martian air for a change!"

"Ha!" she shot back. "Just for that, you can go up first today. Let's see how fast you climb. And I'm going to be right behind you, nagging you to go faster!"

Barbara and Wendy, the two lead members of the repair crew, laughed. "Tell him, sister!" Barbara said.

Patrick threw his hands up good-naturedly. "I surrender! All right, I'll take the lead. But I want you to double-check your tool belt—I'm not going to climb back down because you forgot to bring your wrench!"

They had farther to go this morning. When Sean

and Alex hopped down from the transport, they were higher in the foothills than before. This time the sun shone from a clear sky, and although he knew it wasn't doing much to warm him, Sean quickly felt as though the day were sweltering. Like Leslie, he had more aches and pains than he'd expected, and he had to take it slowly, stopping to rest more often than he had the day before. Alex, behind him, didn't complain at all. Sean supposed he welcomed the rest breaks too.

The first windmill needed only a bearing replacement. They removed the blade assembly, pulled the old bearings, replaced them with new ones, and then reattached the blades. It was a simple job. Then they climbed down again and sat on the Martian surface with their backs against the windmill struts, resting and feeling the steady vibration of the vanes turning far above them. "That's four we've done," Alex said. "And some of the crews did that many yesterday. At this rate, we'll only have a couple to do tomorrow."

"I hope so," Sean confessed. "Another whole day of this would just about finish me off."

"I was waiting for you to say that," Alex announced.

"Why?"

"So I could say, 'Me too!'"

Sean laughed a little at that. "So what was it like for you back on Earth?" he asked. "You stay with your parents?"

"What?"

Sean repeated the question.

Alex turned to look at him, his eyes puzzled behind the plastic helmet. "Are you kidding, or what?"

"What do you mean?" Sean asked.

Alex chuckled. "Man. All the kids in the Asimov Project are orphans, Sean. You didn't know that?"

"But I saw pictures of Roger's mom and dad—"

"They died years ago." Dust was rising along the road. Alex stood up. "Here comes our ride."

Sean got to his feet. "Why are all the kids—"

"Because that way your parents don't have to

grieve if Mars kills you," Alex said. "Not that we'd ever let that happen, of course."

Sean felt strange. He had just assumed that he was the only orphan in the Asimov Project. He found himself wondering what had happened to Jenny's mom and dad: How old had she been? Did she remember them? He wondered what it would be like to have parents, parents that you really knew, and then lose them.

He had often tried to force his memory back to the time when he had a mother and father, but he never could. The earliest thing he could recall was a man holding him up, and another one taking him onto a helicopter. U.S. Army counter-terrorist specialists, taking the few survivors of the Aberlin massacre to safety.

Nothing earlier than that. No home, no mom, no dad.

The transport rattled to a stop, a fine drift of dust catching up with it and settling as they climbed aboard. The driver switched radio frequencies and his voice crackled into their helmets: "One more today. Meteorology's saying there's a high chance of dust storms. We're heading back early."

"Suits me," Alex said.

They sat opposite each other. Sean wanted to ask Alex about his parents, but he couldn't bring himself to do it. It was hard to be the only person on Mars who had no real history. And besides, he didn't want Alex upset, not when they had to climb to the top of yet another tower.

They reached the windmill, and Alex clucked his tongue. "Man, this is another blade job. Mind if I go first this time?"

"Be my guest."

Sean paused to look up. This one would be tough. The blades of the windmill were mangled; one of them had caught in the framework of the tower, one was snapped off short. He waited while Alex hooked his safety line on and started up, and then he followed, ten feet behind.

Above him, Alex's legs pumped steadily as

he climbed the ladder. Sean tried to keep up, but he had to rest more often than Alex did. He felt embarrassment again. Had he been holding things up? Probably, he decided. Alex had been too polite to call him on it.

"Wait up," he said at last, when Alex was far above him.

"Ice. I'm ready for a rest anyway."

Sean toiled up the ladder. When he reached Alex, he heard the other boy whistle. "Sean, we're going to have to unhook to get past this. Be careful, okay?"

Looking up, Sean could see that the badly bent lower blade of the windmill had thrust itself through the framework on the far side and stuck out a couple of feet on their side—right through the ladder. The wind had all but wrapped the tip of the blade around the rail, and it was so tightly jammed that the safety lines would have to be unhooked, then refastened once they were past the obstacle.

"Take it easy, Alex," Sean warned.

"Got it. Here we go. If I fall, catch me."

It took Sean a second to realize that was just a humorless little joke. There would be no catching if the worst should happen.

He saw Alex cautiously unclip his safety line, climb two more rungs, and then hook on again. "Watch the end of the blade. It's sharp enough to cut your pressure suit."

Sean swallowed and followed Alex up. He reached the point where the blade thrust through and saw that the dust, or something, had broken the tip off and had honed the metal sharp as a knife. He felt some misgiving. What would happen when they took the blade assembly off at the top? He didn't know if they could work the blade out from where it was lodged. Maybe they should wait—

No, this was their job. And he wanted to do it well. Sean unhooked his safety line, telling himself that he had never needed it so far. Climbing up five or six feet without it was no big deal.

Sean forced himself not to look down; he couldn't afford to be dizzy. He edged over, avoiding the sharp end of the blade. Thinking that he was already past the blade, he stepped back over—but his boot came to rest not on the rung, but on the point of the windmill blade. He felt himself slip, and he desperately clung to the ladder, hoisting himself by his arms.

He got his foot onto the next rung and let out a deeply held breath. From above: "You okay, Sean?"

"Fine. Let's go."

They made the rest of the climb. Because of the bent and jammed blade, Alex had to edge around the catwalk to the right instead of the left. Sean got to the top, reached to his belt, and took out the pulley. "I don't think we're going to be able to lower this one," he said.

"You may be right," Alex replied. "The shaft looks bent too, and I think the nacelle may be damaged. This is going to be a major overhaul. We'll let them know, but let's see if we can get the blades down. That'll be a start."

The nose cone was pointing down at a fifteen-degree angle, a sure sign that the axle was bent. Alex leaned far out and tried to turn the cone. It was stuck. "A little help here, Sean."

Sean hooked his leg around a strut and leaned out. The nose cone wouldn't give at all. "Let me get a lever through it," he said. He reached to his belt and pulled out a steel rod. It slipped through two holes drilled near the tip of the nose cone, ordinarily closed by two hinged plastic flaps. In an emergency, though, the rod could be pressed through, serving as a handle.

"Ready?" Sean asked. "On three. One, two, three!"

They both shoved, and finally the cap began to rotate. They got it off and let it fall, then hooked on the pulley and the line. "Brake on?" Alex asked.

"Check."

Sean took the bolts nearest him, and Alex worked on the three on his side. They removed the last two at the same time. Sean was leaning far out, his arm hooked around the broken-off stub of the top blade.

Then it happened. The assembly swung free—and

dragged Sean with it. Too late, he remembered that he had not refastened his safety line.

He desperately clutched the hub and upper blade. The pulley brake was not meant to hold his weight along with the blades. He felt it giving, the line screeching through the pulley. Now he was dangling three hundred meters above the surface, clutching the blade, feeling himself beginning to slip. His head reeled, and pure terror made him hold on with a death grip.

"Hang on!" Alex shouted. He had ducked past the nacelle and was grabbing for the line.

The blade swung to the side, threatening to dump Sean off. Below him, the lower blade, weakened where it had bent through the framework, was crumpling.

Alex was grunting, hauling on the line, dragging the blades and Sean back toward the tower. Sean realized that he was just close enough to the framework to grab it—if he could overcome his panic and force his hands to let go of the blade.

"Now!"

For a sickening second, Sean felt himself falling, but his flailing hand grabbed a cross strut. He thudded against the tower, hooked a leg through the maze of struts, and hung there gasping. Alex let go of the line. It fed through the pulley, the brake weakened, and the windmill blades fell outward. There was a shuddering snap. Somewhere below them the lower blade had broken off short. The rest of the assembly plunged down to the surface.

"Give me your safety line," Alex commanded.

It took every bit of nerve that Sean could summon, but he pulled the line out of its reel and passed it up. Alex fastened it into the track with a click. "Now give me your hand."

In a few seconds, Sean was back atop the tower, his head spinning. "I owe you big, man."

"Ice," Alex said with a sickly grin. "Man, look back there." He pointed.

In the far distance Sean could see the writhing form of a dust devil, far south of Marsport. "They're starting early today."

"Better get down."

The descent was hard. Sean's knees kept wanting to give way. By the time they reached the bottom of the ladder they could see the transport speeding up the rutted road toward them.

"Jenny was right," Sean said. "I could've killed myself up there."

"Could've but didn't," Alex said. "Could've been me just as well. But stay sharp. Be better tomorrow."

"You want to partner me again?" Sean asked, surprised.

"Yeah, sure. You just forgot for a second, that's all. You won't do it again. I know from now on you're going to remember."

"What, to latch my safety line?"

"No," Alex said. "That Mars has a million ways to kill you. That's all."

6.1

To Sean's relief, in the days that followed Alex never so much as mentioned the accident. It took them another two days to finish the repairs, and then some of it had to be done over again when another dust devil took out six more of the windmills. On the third morning of the repair mission, Sean had doubted that he would be able to make the long, frightening climb again, but once he had gotten started he had found the ascents were actually a little easier. At least his achy muscles were in better shape. And Alex had been right about one thing: Sean did not forget his safety line again.

With full power restored at last, lessons began again. Dr. Ellman leaned hard on them all to make up for lost time in their physical science sessions, and he was quick to threaten Sean with a forced return to Earth if he fell behind.

Fortunately Nickie Mikhailova seemed to take pity on Sean and tutored him in math and chemistry. It wasn't really her fiel; she was a computer specialist, and she had even built her own personal computer—a tiny voice-activated thing the size of a paperback book—from scratch. Still, she knew a lot about science, and with her drilling him and Jenny Laslo prodding him, Sean began to make some sense of the equations and the strange symbols. He even began to pull off experiments with no virtual explosions, something that he welcomed even if the development seemed to disappoint Mickey Goldberg, who complained more than once that the fireworks display had been postponed again.

Sean fell more and more into the rhythm of life in Marsport. After more than a full month on Mars, he began to sleep better. All the Martian clocks automatically compensated for the difference between an Earth day and a Martian one. Each

Martian hour was a little more than a minute and a half longer than an Earth hour, and there were twenty-four hours in a Martian day, just as in an Earth day. Still, for someone newly arrived from Earth, the extra minute and a half added up. It was as if each day went on a little too long. For the first few weeks, newcomers to Mars felt constantly jet-lagged, as if they were out of synch and out of step with everyone else. And they were, because their biological clocks were slow to adjust.

But gradually the human body was able to get used to the new "day," and finally Sean began to feel like his old self. He was no longer waking up tired, anyway. The sessions in the gym gradually became easier to bear as he built up muscle and endurance. The dreary sameness of the food became more tolerable, and the occasions when fresh, greenhouse-grown vegetables hit the tables were times for celebration. Sean even began to feel at home in the low gravity, no longer reeling and tripping at unexpected moments, but adopting the same kind of loose-limbed walk as the long-time colonists.

But though he still felt like an outsider—Mickey Goldberg in particular was still hounding him about settling on an area of specialization—Sean found that he was indeed fitting in, after a fashion. Like the rest of the colonists, he found himself pausing every evening at 19:35 hours to watch the news transmission from Earth, the narrow-beam cast that gave the colonists a one-hour glimpse of home.

It was seldom good news. More wars, more terrorist attacks, more disease and destruction. Politicians complaining and posturing, but little evidence of anything being done. "I don't believe it's that bad," Alex said one evening after a particularly depressing news program. "I think this must be Earth's way of making us happy to be away from it all. Keeps us from getting homesick and wanting to go back."

Sean started to tell him that he doubted the governments of Earth would hold together for even one more year, but he stopped himself. He didn't know how to explain his inner certainty, and he didn't want to try. He just said, "I'll never go back."

"You wish," Mickey Goldberg said from across the common room. "You'll be out of here before you know it, Doe. You've got to pass every course to stay eligible as a colonist, and you're right on the borderline with a couple. Last week I heard Ellman saying he can't wait to ship you out when the *Argosy* leaves orbit in a month and a half."

Sean glowered at him. "I don't care what Ellman says. Amanda—I mean, Dr. Simak—won't send me back."

"Maybe, maybe not," Mickey said with a grin. "She doesn't have the final word, you know. It's a committee decision, and Dr. Ellman is on that committee. But I really can see her point about bringing you to Mars. I guess maybe it helps to have a celebrity here. You know something, though? I haven't seen your name on the newscasts, so you're not worth much in that department, either."

"Shut it down, Goldberg," Alex said. "You're just

flapping your mouth to make a breeze. Hey, you going to take the Bradbury run in two weeks?"

Mickey rolled his eyes. "Is Jupiter a planet?"

Sean looked at Alex. "What's the Bradbury run?"

"Chance to fly, man," Alex said with a broad smile. "A pilot trainee like me wouldn't miss it. Hey, why don't you sign up to come along? There'll be room. Maybe we can take the same plane."

"Where do we fly?" Sean asked.

Mickey laughed and leaned forward in his chair, spreading his hands theatrically. "Now, see, that's what I'm talking about. Didn't they tell you about the ice meteorites on the trip out?"

Sean responded from memory. "Sure, the ones that hit around the south pole. They come in from Ganymede."

"The Bradbury Project," Mickey said. "Know what that is?"

Sean did. "The plan to enrich the atmosphere of Mars with the liquids and gases from the meteors. After ten or twelve more years, the air will be thick enough to create a strong greenhouse effect. The climate all over Mars will warm up. Then all the ice at the south polar region will melt during the southern summer and create liquid water—it won't just sublime directly to vapor. Eventually we'll even get rain, maybe rivers and lakes."

"The boy can be taught," Mickey said. "Okay, right so far. Now, here's the news flash that you didn't get, Doe. The mass driver on Ganymede is like a big gun. It uses magnetic acceleration instead of gunpowder, but it basically shoots huge bullets of ice into space. The bullets loop around Jupiter, then spiral inward toward the sun and toward Mars. After a long time, they crash near the Martian south pole. But what happens if the gun isn't aimed right?"

"Then the meteors miss Mars, I guess," Sean said.

"Yeah, or they come smashing right into the middle of Marsport. So twice a year we do a Bradbury run to the South Pole. We take readings on the trajectories of incoming meteorites. If we have to adjust the mass driver, the signal has to be sent right now—it takes years for those meteorites to get to us, and if they start to creep north of where they're supposed to land, we have to correct that right away. Otherwise, the meteorites miss us altogether, which is bad, or they hit us, which could be a little bit worse."

"It's a lot of fun, flying to the pole. So what do you say, Sean? You coming with us?" Alex asked.

"What do I have to do?"

Mickey gave a triumphant squawk of laughter, leaned back in his chair, and clapped his hands. "Not much, Doe. Just pull out a 3.75 or better!"

Sean groaned. That was an A average on schoolwork. Exams were coming up. At the moment, Sean had a 3.9 in English and history, but only a 3.5 in life sciences. Even worse, Mickey was right about Sean's two borderline subjects. His math grade was only a 2.4 and his physical science score a barely passing 2.0. "I'll never make it!"

"You don't have to have an *overall* average of

3.75," Alex said, shooting a look at Mickey. "You just have to average that high on the exams. With a little intensive cramming, you can do it. Look, Sean, you probably have like a 3.2 right now. You'll just have to study extra hard for the math and the science, and you've got it."

"Give it up, Benford," Mickey said. "A slow-brain like Doe? He'll never do it."

And right then and there, Sean determined that he *would* do it, if only to prove Mickey wrong.

That started several days of exhaustive studying, drilling, and memorization. Jenny helped a lot, going over and over his life sciences assignments with him until he had the basics down cold. And Nickie, who was very good in math, was glad to step up her tutoring. Sean began to feel as if he was just a learning machine, packing facts, equations, theories, definitions, and more into his brain. But it wasn't easy, not at all, and Sean never felt truly confident. Despite the extra work he put in, he still struggled with math, and he doubted that he'd ever really understand chemistry and physics. But now and then a little light glimmered.

Exam week arrived. A tired but triumphant Sean breezed through English with a perfect 4.0, and came close in history, missing only one item on a long and exhausting test for a 3.99. Jenny had drummed more biology into his head than he thought it could hold, and he didn't do badly on his life sciences exam, winding up with a respectable 3.74. Through the three-hour math test, Sean sweated almost as much as he had climbing the windmill towers, and learned at last that Nickie's tutoring had paid off: He scored a 3.66. That left only natural sciences, Ellman's exam.

Jenny whispered, "You've just got to get a 3.36. You can do it!"

Dr. Ellman had made out twenty different exams,

one for each of his students. He sat at the central desk and gave them all the signal to begin.

Sean turned on his computer and felt his heart sink. The exam was heavily weighted toward chemistry—his worst subject. But he waded in, trying desperately to remember the chart of the elements, ionic potentials, and what a mole was. Some of it came floating back to his consciousness as he worked through the test. He had to skip some of the more difficult problems, rushing ahead to answer the easier questions, then going back to concentrate on the puzzlers.

An hour left. Then thirty minutes. Sean feverishly worked to solve chemical equations, tried to come up with definitions for terms that he was shaky on, took a few guesses when he just didn't know the answer for certain. Fifteen minutes left, then ten.

Finally the screen froze in the middle of Sean's entering an answer. "Time's up," Ellman announced. "I'll score your examinations now."

Sean took a deep breath. He hadn't even begun on

three of the postponed problems, and he wasn't sure how well he'd performed on the ones he did answer. At least he didn't have to suffer a prolonged period of waiting.

The exam had taken three hours. It took only one second for Sean's hopes to be dashed. His score showed up in bright, glowing yellow figures: 3.34. It was a decent B. It would even pull his shaky average in physical sciences up to a fairly steady C.

But it wasn't quite enough.

Sean slapped the desk in annoyance.

"I can dock a few points for misbehavior," Ellman said sharply. He glanced at his own monitor, which gave him a readout of all the grades in the class. "Well, look at that. Mr. Doe, I don't understand your impatience. You did very well. Congratulations."

Sean clamped his jaws shut. All the other students filed out, except for him and Alex. Sean sat slumped in his chair and stared sullenly at the stupid numbers, two one-hundredths of a point too low. Alex came up behind him, bent over his shoulder, and said, "My man!"

"I needed a 3.36," Sean growled.

"Oh, really? Move over."

Alex called up a calculator program and fed in Sean's scores. The result was 3.746.

"I'm still short," Sean pointed out.

"Well, you're lucky that the grading program goes two decimal places and rounds up, aren't you?" Alex asked. The display flickered to round the figures up, and there it was, a big, beautiful 3.75.

6.3

"I'm going, Goldberg!" Sean crowed that afternoon at dinner. "3.75! Read it and weep!"

Mickey shrugged. "Lucked out, did you? Well, I got a 3.88, for your information, so don't get too full of yourself. But I guess I'd be scrambling too if I was afraid of being shipped out." He paused.

"Good going, Doe." His tone was grudging.

"Thanks," Sean said.

And then Mickey added, "If you're taking the Bradbury run, see if you can fly with Alex. I don't want you getting airsick in any cabin with me."

Jenny came in, and Sean jumped up from his table, momentarily forgetting the low gravity. He recovered his balance and carried his tray over to her table, beaming from ear to ear as he sat down next to her. "Thanks for everything. I did it!" he said. "Skin of my teeth, but I squeaked it out! I'm going with you."

"Going with me?" Jenny asked with a frown. "Where do you think I'm going?"

"The Bradbury run," Sean said. "You know—" He broke off in confusion as Jenny's face turned bright red. "What's wrong?"

"I'm not going on the Bradbury run," Jenny said. "I don't qualify. I thought you knew. I'm lousy at history. I've only got a 3.70 on the exams."

"What? But if it's just history—I thought—you're so smart!" Sean spluttered.

She gave him an angry look, and he saw tears in her eyes. "In biology! But I'm scrambling to keep up in everything else. If you weren't so wrapped up in yourself, you might—oh, never mind."

"What's wrong?" Sean asked. "I didn't mean to—"

Jenny was looking down. Tears fell into her lap. "I'm so scared," she whispered. "Everyone else here is so smart, and I'm so dumb. I feel like a fake. Every time we take an exam, I'm sure I'm going to wash out and be sent back to Earth."

"That's just how—" Sean broke off. "Hey, you don't have to worry. You're brilliant at biology. They'd never—anyway, all the teachers like you."

Jenny still wouldn't meet his gaze. "I don't care what happens. I'm not going back to the orphanage."

"What?" Sean asked. "You didn't have a—"

"A family? I'm a Skinner kid," she said bitterly. "They never let us be adopted."

"I don't understand," Sean said. "What's that mean?"

She wiped her eyes, looked around guiltily, and then said, "You really don't know? Okay, put it this way: My mother was a criminal. She died in prison when I was five years old. The government takes kids like me and puts them in Skinner orphanages. They experiment on us."

Sean felt cold. "Do you mean—"

Jenny waved a hand. "Not Frankenstein stuff. No medical experiments. Social ones, education, that kind of thing. We can't transfer out of the orphanage system until we're eighteen. We're like . . . like lab rats or something."

"But you got out. You were selected to come to Marsport," Sean said.

"Charity case," she said bitterly. "I qualified so well in science that they put my name in the lottery for the first round of Asimov Project selections, and I won. Now I have to scramble all the time, but I'm not going back to that. I'm not!"

Sean said, "Look, you're the smartest kid I know. Maybe not in subjects, but in knowing what it's all about. You don't have to be afraid. They'll never send you home, not in a million years."

"That's what you think, just because you don't have anything to worry about," Jenny said. "Amanda Simak is your adopted mother. You're safe. You don't know what it's like for the rest of us."

"You're wrong about that," Sean protested. "Look, I've felt the same way as you do ever since I got here. I mean, I thought I was the dumbest person on the face of the planet. And you're wrong about Amanda. If the committee decided to get rid of me—well, they could send me home any time they wanted to. Right now Ellman's itching to put me aboard the *Argosy,* and I don't know how Mpondo feels about me. That's why I'm always so scared of messing up. I just . . . I never thought that anyone else would be as afraid of being kicked out as I am."

"Well, you were wrong." Jenny smiled weakly.

Sean reached across the table and patted her

hand. She turned her hand over and clasped his. From that moment on Sean knew that, whatever happened, he had at least one friend on Mars he could talk to about anything.

CHAPTER 7

Sean's pilot was Jimmy Carlson, a short, swaggering man with a welcoming grin and a sense of fun and adventure. To his relief—as well as to Mickey's, he was sure—Sean learned that his partner would be Roger Smith, the youngest of the Asimov Project kids. As they waited for a preflight briefing, Roger congratulated Sean on qualifying for the trip.

"I heard you got a 4.0," Sean replied. "That's impressive."

"Well, it was a 3.996, actually, but they rounded up," Roger said simply. He wasn't bragging, Sean realized. Roger just loved to be exact about figures. "Is it true that you were a survivor of the Aberlin massacre?" he asked.

"Yeah," Sean grunted. "But I don't remember anything about it. I don't even remember my parents."

"My parents were both doctors who were killed while helping in the Pan-African war," Roger said. "I was nine at the time."

For a few moments they sat in silence, waiting for their pilot in the hangar dome where three airplanes were docked. They looked almost nothing like Earth jets to Sean. The bodies of the planes were sleek and silvery, the engines relatively tiny, and the wings were enormous, as they had to be in the thin atmosphere of Mars.

"Did you bring your tele helmet?" Roger asked.

"My what?"

"Tele helmet," Roger said, with a surprised glance. But then Roger *always* looked surprised, his eyebrows permanently arched high on his forehead. "You know, the little fold-up hood that transmits whatever you see back to the ship? We're required to have one."

"I don't have one," Sean said. "Nobody told me."

"Expect they thought you'd find it in the manual," Roger told him with a shrug.

"Manual?" Sean asked, suddenly feeling nervous.

"Yes, the flight manual. Didn't you pick yours up?"

Sean shook his head. "Where was I supposed to—"

"In the Prep Dome, when you took your preflight med tests."

"Preflight med tests?"

"Yes, the ones that we were told about in the transmission last week."

"What transmission?" Sean asked, panicked.

"The one that came over your tele helmet, of course," Roger said reasonably.

Sean wailed, "But I don't *have* a—" He broke off and glared at Roger.

"Gotcha," Roger said, giggling.

Sean rolled his eyes. That was another thing he had learned about Roger. If Roger was the least bit bored, he could think up intricate little jokes. And people almost invariably fell for them.

"Sorry I'm late, guys!" Jimmy Carlson hurried in, his orange uniform crisp and neat. He wasn't much taller than Sean, but his compact frame seemed to hold enough energy for five or six people. "Okay, listen up. The ship we'll be taking is the MAR/S-7. That stands for—"

"Martian Aerial Reconnaissance/Survey craft," Roger said promptly.

"Right! Ordinarily, these ships can carry a pilot, copilot, and six passengers. Because we're hauling some equipment as well, it'll just be me, our copilot and navigator Sara Havasian, and the two of you. We'll have ten different survey spots where we'll set down, take instrumental readings, and then wait for a visual observation of meteor trajectories. We'll be out six days in all, with basic rations and water, along with a reasonable amount of emergency survival gear. I hope you guys can sleep in a reclined seat and don't mind sharing a chemical john with three other people, because that's the situation."

He looked at his watch. "Okay, you'll need to be

familiar with five different types of instruments. I want you to spend the next couple of days studying them on your computers, and then we'll do a couple of days of training. Assuming you get through that okay, we'll plan for takeoff at 6:00 hours Monday. Heck of a way to spend your school vacation, isn't it?"

They toured the aircraft—it was going to be very tight, Sean saw—and learned about the emergency gear: a heated tent with a small oxygen generator, compressed food rations, a global positioning monitor and location beacon, and a radio. "You'll have to wear these," Jimmy said, handing Sean and Roger each a small device like an old-fashioned wristwatch. "Key in your ID numbers now. Do it twice to confirm them."

They did, and Sean saw the face of his device register his name, age, and dorm room assignment. "Are these GPS locators, too?" he asked.

"Right," Jimmy told him. "Mars doesn't have as complete a satellite grid as Earth, but as long as you're wearing this device, the satellites we do have can track you to within fifty meters or so. If we get stranded, a rescue craft can find us and bring us back."

"For burial," Roger said cheerfully.

Jimmy winked. "Never happens," he said. "Well, almost never."

The instruments that Sean had to learn about proved to be pretty simple. They were almost all robotic—that is, they were computerized with high levels of artificial intelligence, and they "knew" their jobs. The crew's main task would be to ferry the instruments to the correct locations, set them up, and let them perform their functions. Sean thought that the actual work of the expedition wouldn't be nearly as hard as studying for his exams had been.

There were five ships in all, each with a four-person crew. Other than Roger and Sean, nine students were going along on the expedition. Alex was partnered with Nickie, Mickey Goldberg with Leslie. The remaining two aircraft would be on the far side of the south polar icecap.

All nine students did their practice instrument setups under the supervision of David Czernos, the lead areologist of Marsport. His specialty was the structure and chemical composition of the Martian regolith, the rock that made up the planet, but he was keenly interested in the meteorology and planetography of Mars as well. "Have to call it planetography," he explained to the students as they stood on the surface just past the landing strip. "The *geo-* in geography means 'Earth,' and Mars is not Earth, right?"

It was a warm day for Mars. The temperature at their location, south of Olympus Mons, was 14 degrees Celsius, or 57 degrees Fahrenheit. "All right. First let's do the check for subsurface water. Mr. Goldberg, what instrument do we use?"

Mickey correctly produced the device, a seismic

scanner no larger than a small aquarium. He demonstrated how to set it up and activate it. The machine operated perfectly, and Czernos showed them a holographic readout. "Very little water under us here, see? That's because Marsport is built on more or less solid rock. Permafrost exists in more porous areas. All right, Ms. Mikhailova, I want to track an incoming meteor. How do I do it?"

Nickie set up a computerized theodolite, an instrument that measured horizontal and vertical angles.

The training period continued. They went through each instrument package one by one, and then each student demonstrated that he or she knew how to set up all of the measuring devices.

"Good, good," Czernos said when they had all finished. "All right. Get a good night's sleep tonight, and be sure to take a shower. You won't have another chance for nearly a week—unless we find a heated lake at the south pole, and so far they've eluded us."

That evening Sean found Jenny and told her about

preparing for the expedition. They sat in the library dome, where Jenny, as usual, was poring over texts taken from the main library computer. The library wasn't crowded. With a three-week school holiday, the students who weren't going on the Bradbury run were kicking back and relaxing, not hitting the books.

"Good thing you got to go," she said with a rueful smile. "Sounds like you're really going to like it."

"I wish you could come too," Sean told her.

She shrugged. "Maybe next time, if I can pull up my history grade."

"I can tutor you, if you want," Sean told her.

"I'd like that," Jenny said. "Thanks."

When he left her, Sean couldn't stop grinning. All those years on Earth of hiding, of fighting with other kids for scraps of food, hadn't prepared him for this. Jenny liked him, and he liked her. He was beginning to think there wasn't anything he couldn't do, provided he had a few friends along.

"All right, crew," Jimmy Carlson said from the cockpit. "We're next for takeoff, so hold on to something that won't bend or break."

Sara Havasian, taller than Jimmy and a few years younger, was all business in the copilot's seat. "Flight path locked in," she said. "Final instrument check completed."

Roger leaned toward Sean and whispered, "I hope you packed your tele helmet."

Sean chuckled despite himself.

Then they were moving, trundling out onto the runway and picking up speed as they headed to the south. The airplane lifted off, tilted sharply, and soared up into the Martian air. The sky rapidly became a deeper, richer blue, and the horizon showed a distinct curve. Mars was a much smaller planet than Earth, and you didn't have to get very far above it before the air thinned and you were able to see that it was a sphere.

"We'll be flying at about ten thousand meters most of the way," Jimmy said as they leveled off. "I'll show you a few of the sights."

Sean looked out the window at the bleak landscape below. Except for five or six scientific outposts, the only human habitation on the face of Mars was Marsport. Everywhere else the landscape was wild, rugged, and barren. Impact craters millions of years old showed where meteorites had slammed into the planet. More volcanoes, like Olympus Mons but nowhere near as huge, loomed here and there. They flew over Valles Marineris, named for one of the first Earth probes to visit Mars. It was an enormous canyon, a split in the face of the planet.

"People used to call that the Grand Canyon of Mars," Jimmy said cheerfully. "Not a very good description. Valles Marineris is four thousand kilometers long; on Earth, it would stretch from California to Washington, D.C. It's deep, too. Parts of its floor are ten kilometers below the surface plain.

When we get water on Mars, that's going to be one long, deep lake!"

Sean could hardly imagine the canyon full of water. It was sheer-sided in places, and in others he saw slopes that looked like ancient landslides. "They say you can walk around down there without a breathing mask," Roger told him. "You could survive for maybe five or ten minutes if you were at the bottom of the canyon."

"That's not very long," Sean said.

"No," Roger agreed thoughtfully. "But it would be an *interesting* five or ten minutes!"

Sean closed his eyes and somehow dozed off. When he woke up again, Roger was nudging him. "We're coming in," he said. "Brace yourself for the landing."

"I resent that," Jimmy shot back with a smile. "My landings are perfect."

Sean looked down. It was still day, but the shadows beneath the plane were long. They were passing over a relatively flat plain, studded with boulders and rock outcroppings. In the shadows something white gleamed. "Ice?" Sean asked.

Sara craned to look down. "Frozen carbon dioxide," she said. "It's cold down there, guys. Even in the pressure suits you can't stay outside the ship for very long."

"Here we go," Jimmy said, and the plane tilted as they lost altitude.

The surface came closer, and rocks and hills flashed past. "It's going to be quite a chore, dodging these boulders," Roger said.

"We're shooting for a prepared landing strip," Jimmy told him. "If we're lucky, we might even find it. There we go, navigation beam acquired. Hang on. It's a short field and a sudden stop."

The MAR/S-7 touched down and rolled along at a tremendous speed, jouncing and shuddering. Dust rose outside the windows as the plane braked, and Sean felt himself thrust forward, the lap and shoulder belt pressing into him as the craft came to a stop.

"Not bad," Sara said dryly. "We still have nearly two meters of field left."

"Okay, suit up, one at a time," Jimmy said. "Sara first, and then you guys. We'll make sure the plane is secure, then set up the instruments for the first reading. I hope you enjoy this. It's going to be the same routine for the next five days!"

The next day Sean realized that Jimmy wasn't kidding. They had moved a few hundred kilometers to another short strip, where they had gone outside, again, and had set up the instruments, again. The pale sun rode very low on the horizon. In the southern hemisphere of Mars, the season was mid-autumn. The days were short and getting shorter. In a few months the polar night would set in, and then the sun would not rise at all until spring came again.

To the south the sky shaded away to a deep indigo, where a few stars glittered even during the hours of sunlight. Frost, both ice and frozen carbon dioxide, spiked up in the shelter of every rock and ridge. And

Sara had been right: The heated pressure suits did little to keep out the chill. Half an hour was about as much as they could take at a time.

The first day's observations had been normal. On the second day, they waited to glimpse a meteorite, one of the frozen balls of water and gas coming in from Ganymede. It should, if all was well, pass well to the south of them, but Jimmy said it would be a sight to see.

The satellite system did a good job of tracking incoming meteors, and they knew just when and where to look. Sean stood on the surface, head tilted back, staring out through the plastic bubble of his helmet. He tried to ignore the creeping cold in his toes.

"Here it comes!" Sara said, pointing.

Sean caught sight of it: a brilliant, glowing white streak against the cold, dark blue sky. The meteor was coming in at a shallow angle and would go halfway around the globe, mostly disintegrating before its icy core crashed to the surface, but it was low enough for Sean to see the clouds of vapor boiling off it. It left behind a spreading canopy of cloud, so white on the sunward side that it almost hurt to look at it, shading to a deep gray on the far side. The cloud billowed and grew, swelling until it filled half the sky.

And just when Sean's toes were beginning to ache unbearably from the cold, it began.

Sean had to tilt his head just right to see them, but glittering crystals were swirling down from the sky.

"There you go," Jimmy said. "A miracle."

Roger laughed and held out his gloved hand. White specks appeared on the orange fabric.

Not rain. Not yet. Not for perhaps decades.

But right here, right now, it was snowing on Mars.

CHAPTER 8

8.1

Near the end of the Bradbury run, Sean was in the MAR/S-7, taking his turn as the ship monitor, keeping an eye on the seismic, meteorological, and astronomical readings the instruments were beaming back to Marsport. It was a boring job, and he wished he could be outside with the others.

And then the MW receiver suddenly came to life, with Mickey Goldberg's frightened voice calling, "We need help!"

Sean turned on the transmitter. "Ship eight, this is seven. What's wrong?"

"Sean? Listen, we've crashed! We've got an air leak—they're trying to seal it now, but we're losing oxygen fast. We have two hurt. Get us out of here!"

Sean looked at the locator screen and saw that it

was showing nothing. "Turn on your beacon. I'll round up our crew. Get the beacon on now!"

He changed frequencies and quickly told Jimmy, Sara, and Roger the news. They hurriedly gathered their instruments and returned to the ship. Sean heard the airlock cycling as he went back to the MW transponder. "Mickey, get your locator beacon going. I can't pick you up."

"It's on!" Mickey's voice was more frightened than ever. "You should be able to see us. Wait a minute, let me get our GPS coordinates."

Sean waited, hearing the rest of the crew open the inner door of the airlock. Before they reached the cockpit, Mickey read off a string of figures. Sean entered them into the navigation computer and commanded the machine to fix the position. An instant later a detailed holographic map shimmered into existence above the computer panel. The MAR/S-7 was at the eastern end of the Aonian Plain. Mickey and the MAR/S-8 were hundreds of kilometers away at the western end.

Jimmy slipped into the pilot's seat and checked the map. "We're closest. Secure for takeoff, everyone. Good work, Sean."

Sean got to his seat. Roger had a hundred questions, and by the time Sean had answered half of them, they were airborne. Sara put out a call to the Bradbury run ships, telling them of the accident and requesting them to stand by in case the MAR/S-7 crew needed assistance.

The flight was a short hop, and before long they angled in for a landing, a rougher one on this side of the plateau. Sean strained to see the MAR/S-8, but he couldn't catch sight of it. Jimmy was on the radio again, talking to Mickey, as their craft braked to a halt. As soon as they had stopped, Jimmy turned to his crew. "Listen up. The MAR/S-8 is about two klicks to the west. They were taking off and didn't make it, and Jappa got them down as best she could, but she and her copilot Rial are both injured, and Mickey and Leslie have set up the survival tent. Sara, you keep watch here. Sean, Roger, suit up. Sean will come with me. Roger, I want you to clear out anything we don't need—tent, emergency supplies, instruments. Sean, grab two oxygen tanks. We may need them."

Two kilometers was a little more than one mile, but to Sean it seemed to take forever to walk it. Once he and Jimmy were off the landing strip, the ground underfoot was strewn with rocks, rolling in a series of low hills, and cut with ancient dry water courses. It was hard going with two oxygen tanks under his arms. Ahead of him, Jimmy carried two tanks plus a bulky medical kit. Sean hoped they would make it to the others in time.

They climbed a fairly high hill and Sean saw the wreckage of the MAR/S-8 ahead. The plane had come down hard and the starboard wing had sheared off. The port wing lay crumpled and half torn from the fuselage. A trail of debris—metal, glass, and plastic—glittered between the ripped-off starboard wing and the rest of the plane. The domed emergency tent was close by the wrecked plane, with a plume of vapor coming from its top vent.

"Looks like they got the oxygen generator going, anyway," Jimmy said. "Come on."

He called for Mickey over his helmet radio, and after a moment, Mickey responded. "Where are you guys?"

"We're with you," Jimmy said, panting a little. "Is everyone in pressure suits?"

"Negative," Mickey said. "The captain's unconscious, and the copilot has a broken arm."

"Okay, we'll use the airlock. It won't be perfect, but we've brought extra oxygen to make up for a leak. We'll have to come in one at a time. Seal up the inside door if you haven't already done it."

They reached the tent. Jimmy opened the outer door flap and then sealed it behind him. "I'm in," Sean heard him say. "Seal shows green. Open the inner door."

Sean saw the outer door flap billow, and a few icy plumes of vapor shot out. As Jimmy had said, the seal wasn't perfect, and the tent had lost a little air.

With his feet feeling frozen, Sean waited.

His helmet transponder came to life: "Sean, this is Jim. Jappa has serious injuries. We have to get her back to Marsport a.s.a.p. Goldberg says the cockpit MW is still operational. Get into the ship and patch your helmet radio into the MW system. Give Sara a call and tell her to taxi the MAR/S-7 off the end of the runway and toward us, slowly. Then I want you to check in the med locker and bring me a body baggie, okay?"

Sean left the two oxygen containers and hurried toward the ship. He ran—which, given the low gravity, meant that he bounded over the surface like an earthly kangaroo. He reached the crashed aircraft and saw that the airlock door was open. That meant the inside of the ship would have no more air than the surface of Mars.

He climbed into the cabin and found the floor tilted crazily to the left. He struggled to the pilot's seat and turned on the MW set.

Sean made his call, and Sara, in a worried tone,

acknowledged. Then Sean crept back down the tilted aisle to the medical locker and opened it. A jumble of equipment fell out. What he wanted was a partly silver and partly clear thick plastic bag with a couple of small tanks attached. The colonists called them body baggies, but actually they were sealed stretchers. Their small auxiliary heaters and oxygen tanks would keep a patient alive on Mars.

At least for a short time.

8.2

The tent huffed out a cloud of fog as Jimmy unsealed the door. Sean was freezing, but there was nothing he could do about that right now. Rial Whitepath, the copilot of the MAR/S-8, crawled out. His face was strained inside the helmet. Jimmy had strapped Rial's broken right arm to his chest, and the right arm of his pressure suit bulged and flapped weirdly. Leslie followed, lugging the foot end of the body baggie, and then came Jimmy, holding the head part. Through the transparent plastic, Sean could see Jappa Nannup's head, bandaged and bruised. She was a small woman, an Aborigine from Australia, and Sean remembered her as always laughing.

Now she looked dead.

"Okay," Jimmy said. "Here's the drill. The MAR/S-7 can transport Jappa, Rial, and Leslie, but Mickey and Sean will have to stay behind here in the tent. The MAR/S-6 will land in another hour, and they'll jettison enough stuff to load the two of you. You have enough oxygen to last for a day, even without the generator, so you should be all right. Rial, can you make it?"

"Yeah," the copilot said in a weak voice.

"Goldberg, Doe, into the tent and repressurize. Listen for the MAR/S-6 crew, but don't expect them for another two hours or so. They'll have to land and then send someone to escort you."

Sean ducked into the tent, and after a moment

a strangely reluctant Mickey followed. Jimmy said, "Outer door sealed."

Sean sealed the inner tent door and said, "Secure here. We'll repressurize."

Jimmy acknowledged, and then he was gone. Sean checked the oxygen generator. Its shaft had been thrust through a valve in the tent floor, then drilled into the soil surface beneath the tent. It was putting out just enough oxygen to allow him and Mickey to breathe, but it would be nearly an hour before the pressure built up enough to let them remove their helmets.

"Let's crack one of the tanks," Sean suggested. "Speed things up a little."

He opened the valve on one of the oxygen tanks he had lugged to the crash site. Within seconds the tent was pressurized with a breathable atmosphere, and Sean took off his helmet with a sense of relief. "What happened?" he asked, his voice sounding strange and thin.

Mickey looked miserable. "We missed a small

crater in the runway when we did our preflight check. It must have been filled in with loose dust. The plane hit it, tilted, and we lost part of the starboard wingtip just as we were taking off. Jappa fought for control, but we couldn't gain altitude, and we had to set down. The ground's uneven, and we cracked up."

"How could you miss a crater?" Sean asked, surprised. That was part of the routine for taking off: You swept the runway with penetrating radar to make sure there were no obstacles in the way.

"I just missed it, okay?" Mickey snapped.

Sean realized what Mickey was trying not to say. The older boy had been careless. He'd been the one entrusted with the runway sweep, and he'd fouled up. For a nasty moment, Sean felt delighted. Mickey was always quick to criticize him. Sean could show him what it felt like to be on the receiving end.

But Sean didn't say anything. Mickey looked miserable enough on his own. "Is the heater working?" Sean asked. His suit heater was on full blast, and still he felt as if he were about to freeze.

"Notched up as high as it'll go," Mickey said. "At this latitude, we can maintain an air temperature of about twelve for a day or two. Then the batteries give out and we freeze in the dark."

On the Aonian Plain they were outside the Antarctic Circle of Mars, and they wouldn't completely lose the sun. But the day was very short, and the shrunken sun gave off little heat. Sean tried to remember what the outside temperature was. Probably seventy-something below zero. Twelve degrees didn't sound so bad, after all.

Mickey didn't want to talk. Half an hour after Jimmy had left, his voice came through on Sean's helmet radio. Sean put the helmet back on to talk to the pilot. "We're okay," he said. "What's up?"

"We're taxiing back to the runway now," Jimmy said. "Jappa is stable, as far as we can tell, but still unconscious. We're going to be heavy, but I think we've got enough lift to get into the air before we hit the far end of the runway. MAR/S-6 is on track to land in, let's see, thirty-four minutes, and they'll pull you and Mickey out. Hang in there, Sean."

"We will."

And then there was nothing to do but wait. Mickey sat huddled and miserable near the center of the tent. Sean couldn't stay still. With nervous, worried energy, he paced around and around the edge of the tent, which meant that he had to bend forward. From time to time he paused and looked out the small round windows. The one facing south showed him a range of terraced hills, glistening white with carbon dioxide and water frost. They rose one above the other until they faded into the polar darkness.

What seemed like hours passed, and then they picked up a call from MAR/S-6. "We've landed, guys," the pilot said. "Two of us will come to lead you back. The other two are going to dump everything we don't need so there'll be room. Sorry to hear about Jappa."

"Well, we're safe," Sean said to Mickey.

"*You* are," the older boy said bitterly.

The flight back to Marsport took hours, and it was doubly uncomfortable for Sean and Mickey. The MAR/S-6 had jettisoned a lot of equipment, but it still had only four seats installed, and no one wanted to take time to move two more from the wrecked plane. Mickey and Sean sat on the deck, hanging on to the seats in front of them for takeoff and landing.

Sean was never as glad to arrive anywhere as he was to step through the airlock and into the hangar back at Marsport. Jenny was there waiting, and she ran forward, relief flooding her face. "You're all right!" she said to Sean and Mickey. "Thank God!"

"I'm frozen into a Doe-sicle, but other than that I'm fine," Sean said. His joints ached with cold, and he felt as if he'd never be warm again. "I hope we got enough data before the crash."

"You did fine," Jenny told him. "The ships have enough readings to show that the mass driver on

Ganymede doesn't need adjusting. Next month some follow-up crews will go out and pick up the equipment you left behind, and they'll finish any observations that you had to leave incomplete. Come on, let's get back to the dorms."

"How's Jappa?" Mickey asked, his voice fretful.

Jenny looked at him, then at Sean. "You haven't heard? She—she didn't make it."

Mickey froze. He glared at her. "You're lying!"

"There was nothing they could do," Jenny said. "I'm sorry."

With a bitter curse, Mickey shoved past them and vanished down a corridor. Sean looked after him. "He thinks it's his fault."

"Was it?" Jenny asked.

"I don't know," Sean told her. "But he thinks it is, and that's bad enough."

"There's worse," Jenny said. "We've lost contact with Earth. Nothing since yesterday morning," she said. "Something terrible's happening there. The Lunatics say they can't raise Earth, either. Luna Base has been monitoring conditions on Earth, and they know there's an economic meltdown. You know history?"

Sean gave her a look.

Jenny's smile was miserable. "Course you do, with your grades. Remember the depression in the middle of the Twentieth Century?"

"Earlier than that," Sean said. "It started in 1929."

"This is a hundred times worse, they say. And there are five or six epidemics going on, and some terrorist activity hitting the power grid, and . . . it looks bad."

They had reached the dorms. No one was in the common area, and Sean and Jenny sat at a table. Sean was frowning. "I felt something like this was coming," he said. "I didn't know exactly what—war, plague, collapse—but I could tell something really bad was brewing. What does that mean for us?"

"The council is talking about evacuating Marsport," Jenny said. "And the Asimov Project kids will be the first to go."

"No," Sean said at once. "Not me."

"And not me," Jenny added. "If things on Earth are as bad as you say they are, there's no point. I'd rather take my chances here. But I know the council has told the *Argosy* to prepare to take on passengers, and the *Magellan* is due to launch from Earth orbit any day now. Between the two of them, if they carry no cargo but passengers, they'd be able to ferry a thousand colonists back to Earth. It'll take three trips, about nine more years, but they could take everyone back eventually."

"I'll leave when Amanda does," Sean said. "Not before."

"Count me in," Jenny said. "I'll be part of your crew."

"The dumb crew?" Sean asked with a bitter smile.

She touched his hand. "The Doe crew," she corrected.

CHAPTER 9

9.1

For one day, Marsport grieved its loss. A brief memorial service for Captain Jappa Nannup was held at noon, and shortly afterward a funeral detail took her body to Marsport Cemetery, where it joined the bodies of a dozen other Mars explorers who had died over the years.

When Sean told Alex that he and Jenny planned to stay on Mars, Alex immediately joined the Doe Crew, and right after that, Roger came over to add his support. Leslie was next, and then Nickie. Sean tried to see Amanda, but found that she was too busy with official meetings. He could understand that, but he wished he could at least speak with her. All the rest of the day, word spread among the teens, and one by one they came to find him. Before lights out that evening, nineteen of the twenty Asimov Project kids had pledged to remain in Marsport, whatever happened.

The following day, the council called an assembly at eleven in the morning. It was an odd kind of assembly, since Marsport had no area big enough for all three thousand colonists to congregate. They gathered in all the common areas instead. Sean's dorm wing common area could barely hold the twenty Asimov Project kids, and nineteen of them gathered there to watch the holoscreen and hear what the council had decided.

A grim-looking Amanda Simak appeared on the screen, flanked by Tim Mpondo and Harold Ellman. "I won't conceal the seriousness of the situation from you," she said without any kind of formal beginning. "Earth is in deep trouble. All indications from the Luna Colony are that an international war has broken out, complicated by economic collapse, widespread disease, and ecological disaster. I frankly don't know whether there is any safe area on the face of the Earth at this moment.

"Our state of affairs is not promising. We are still dependent on twice-yearly shipments of food, medical supplies, and other necessities from Earth orbit. We are on the verge of being self-sustaining. Whether we can become so immediately is an open question."

She paused, letting this sink in. The young people gathered in the common area murmured among themselves. "Maybe she's going to say we might as well stay on," Alex said hopefully. Jenny shushed him.

With a weary, strained expression, Dr. Simak continued: "The council has decided that it's unfair to ask colonists to remain here on Mars, given our uncertain future. Tomorrow, beginning at 8:00 hours, the council will begin accepting applications for a return to Earth. These will be granted on a first-come, first-served basis. I have asked the crew of the *Argosy* to prepare to take as many people back to Earth as they can. When you arrive there, in more than a year's time, you will be ferried down to the surface if that is practicable. If not, Luna Colony has reached self-sustaining status, and they will accept you as refugees. I am told that, at a maximum, the *Argosy* can transport slightly more than six hundred passengers. That gives the ship no margin for error on food and supplies. Even at that, rationing will be tight. I want you all to think about the situation for the rest of the day. Ordinary duties are suspended."

She glanced at Ellman, who stood beside her, his face rigid, showing no emotion. Then, looking back into the camera, Dr. Simak said, "I should have said that one group of colonists will return to Earth whether they apply to go or not. This one exception will be the twenty young people in the Asimov Project. Dr. Ellman has made a strong case that we have no right to expose these colonists to the uncertainties and risks that the rest of us will have to face for at least one full Martian year, until the *Magellan* can reach us and take perhaps another thousand colonists home."

"Home?" exclaimed Leslie. "This *is* home!"

"Therefore," continued Dr. Simak, "the twenty Asimov Project colonists will prepare for evacuation. We expect to begin ferrying the returning colonists to the ship in two days. With luck and hard work, we can load all six-hundred-odd passengers by the end of the week, and the *Argosy* will then leave orbit.

"My fellow colonists, please think very clearly and very seriously about what I have said. Some of us will remain behind, regardless. We will do our best to survive and to become independent of Earth. I think we have at least a fifty-fifty chance of succeeding. It will be hard—I won't hide that from you. The effort will present you with the greatest challenges you have ever faced. Still, I believe that together we can succeed. I know you all very well. I couldn't ask for a better group of people to make a stand with. Thank you."

The holoscreen faded to nothing. For a moment everyone was silent.

Then a new voice broke in: "I'm with you. If you'll have me."

Mickey Goldberg stood in the doorway.

Alex whooped. "Welcome to the Doe crew!" he said. "Now we have to make plans."

"There's nowhere to hide," Jenny insisted in despair. "They can sweep the whole compound in less than a day! Where are we supposed to go?"

"Somewhere they can't find us," Sean insisted. "There has to be a place!"

"The hangars," Mickey suggested. "Maybe we could climb aboard the planes and they wouldn't think to check there."

"We could steal survival tents and go out onto the surface," Nickie volunteered. "We can hang out there until the *Argosy*'s launch window is over."

"No good," Alex said morosely. "If we were in the

hangars, they could use heat sensors to find us. And survival tents are *designed* to be seen from a distance."

"There's Lake Ares," Jenny said slowly. "I think if we all were in pressure suits we could survive under the surface for a few hours. Of course, we'd tend to float, so we'd have to be anchored to something."

"One thing we can do to begin with," Sean said, "is to round up all our wrist locators. The first thing they'll check will be the GPS system. I've got an idea about that."

Alex and Leslie took all twenty of the wrist devices to the point farthest from the dorm wings, the factory domes where the colonists refined steel from the iron in the Martian rocks. They activated all the locators and left them in the observation room on the top of the most distant factory dome, along with a note that they all had signed:

To the Marsport Council:
We have decided to stay on Mars. There is

nothing on Earth for any of us. We believe that since the Asimov Project began four years ago, we have proved our value to the colony and our ability to do our part. If any colonists are going to take a stand here, we want to be part of that stand. We don't want to cause trouble, and we are not rebelling for the sake of rebellion. We ask your acceptance, but with it or without it, we are part of Marsport and will remain here with any colonists who decide to stay.

Mickey Goldberg had shaken his head as he read the note before signing it. "Not exactly the Declaration of Independence, is it?"

"It says what we want to say," Jenny told him. "And what's more important, we've all signed it."

Mickey had added his name, and then the note went into hiding with the wrist locators.

As soon as everyone was together, Sean said, "The room locators are the big problem. We can't play hide-and-seek when each room has sensors that can tell them if people are inside."

"Not necessarily," Jenny said thoughtfully. "There are a couple of corridors that don't have that kind of detector, because they're cut back into the surface of the planet. They were the first storage areas when Marsport was started. Now they're used for emergency supplies—rations, medical stuff, things like that. But we can't get to them without going through the corridors, and we'd be noticed."

"How about the greenhouses?" Patrick asked.

Jenny shook her head. "No good. There's just no cover there. They've got carbon dioxide detectors, and we all have to breathe."

"If we wore pressure suits—"

"We'd have the built-in suit locators," Mickey said wearily.

Sean was thinking furiously. He knew there was a way. But what was it?

"I'm going to get killed for this," Nickie Mikhailova muttered in a despairing voice. She was feverishly working with her private minicomputer. "I think I can tie into the communications net without being detected, but it's against all kinds of rules."

"So's hiding out when you've been ordered to leave the colony," Roger pointed out.

It was late, far past the normal lights-out hour, but colonists all over Marsport were still up, pondering and arguing their choices. Time was running short. In seven hours, it would be 8:00, and at that time the Asimov Project kids were supposed to report to the council to prepare for their evacuation.

Sean paced, as he always did when faced with a serious problem. He kept feeling that he had missed something obvious.

And then he remembered the day that the dust devils had knocked out power to the station. He whirled. "I've got it!" he yelled. Then he bit his lip.

"Nickie, when's the latest possible launch date for the *Argosy*?"

"Five days," Nickie responded at once. "End of the week, just as Dr. Simak said. After that they'd have to delay for months before launching."

"We need emergency rations for five days. How much water will we need at a minimum?"

Jenny shrugged. "Five days? Three liters each would just about see us through."

"Then let's start collecting water. We can't tap into the system, or they could trace us. Okay, I need five people to collect sixty liters of water and five to collect emergency rations. Who's up for it?"

Sean had his pick of volunteers. "Be careful not to get caught," he warned them. "Water committee, collect from *all* the dorm wings—we don't want to make anyone suspicious by taking that much water from one place. Alex, come with me. We have to check something out."

Sean and Alex hurried through the corridors, passing domes where worried adults were still talking about the crisis. No one paid the teens much attention. They reached the tube that led into the tunnels, and there Sean stopped, studying the floor. "How do the service panels lift out?" he asked.

Alex understood at once. "You have to have a code key," he said. "There's an access panel by the door. Punch in the code and the conduit cover hatch opens."

Sean growled in frustration. "I thought I had it!"

"Hang on," Alex said. "I doubt they've changed the codes. I watched some repair work months ago. Let me see if I can remember." He opened the access panel, revealing a keypad. "It was a long time ago," he said doubtfully.

"How many numbers?" Sean asked.

"Four, but—"

Sean studied the pad. This was one of the oldest corridors in the colony, and the pad had been there a long time. The numbers showed uneven wear— and the numbers 1, 5, 8, and 9 had been pressed so many times that the numerals were barely visible.

"Must be a combination of these," Sean said, reading them out.

"That sounds familiar," Alex said. "Think if we try all the combinations we'll trigger an alarm or something?"

"We can't take that chance," Sean said. "What's the trick? There's got to be some reason for those four numbers."

"If it was up to me, I'd spell out the word 'Mars,'" Alex said. "But the only number you could use would be the one, because *M* is the thirteenth letter of the alphabet, *R* is the eighteenth, and *S* the nineteenth."

"That's it!" Sean said excitedly. "I'll bet it does spell 'Mars,' but *you go around twice.* Hang on, let me see." Without quite touching the buttons, Sean recited the alphabet as he pointed to each one. The zero represented *J,* and then he went back to 1 for the *K.* But he pulled up short. "Rats. *M* would be 3, and that one looks practically new compared to the 1, 5, 8, and 9."

"Maybe it's just a random number."

Sean shook his head. "That's not the way colonists think. I mean, look at how they decided to name the airplanes: 'Martian Aerial Reconnaissance/Survey craft,' just so they could get the letters *M*, *A*, *R*, and *S*. I'd bet anything that there's something like that going on here, too."

Alex said thoughtfully, "You know, when we were having our orientation, Dr. Czernos said not to call him a geologist, because 'geo' means 'Earth.' He's an Areologist, because the Greek name for Mars is—"

"Ares," Sean finished. "Let's see—" His pointing finger danced over the keypad again. "It works!" he said. "That would make the code 1895. Does that sound familiar?"

"I think that's it," Alex said.

"I'm going to try it." Sean hesitated for just a second. He took a deep breath and punched the numbers in. They heard a faint click, and Alex knelt and pressed the edge of one of the access panels. It tilted down, and in a moment he had lifted it up, revealing the three-foot-wide conduit.

Alex grinned up at Sean. "This is our way in. There won't be any sensors down in this trench. We can unlatch the panels manually from the inside, and we can even refasten this one. Think it will work?"

"It has to," Sean said. "Let's get the others."

CHAPTER 10

10.1

It was a nerve-racking night. In groups of two and three, each group carrying supplies and water, the Doe Crew slipped through the corridors, taking different routes to the tube outside the tunnels. Then they slipped into the service conduit and crept half the length of a football field to the last storage area, really a cavern blasted out of the bedrock. It was dark, cold, and deserted. This particular storage area held crates of tools.

"Should've brought a heater," grumbled Jenny, hugging herself. "They don't do much to keep these above freezing."

Sean said, "We'll keep close together. Okay, we have to keep watch, and we have to make a few decisions. One is bathroom facilities. We could sneak back into the colony, but I don't think that's a good plan. Any ideas?"

Mickey offered, "Easiest thing to do is to use a couple of chemical pails. We'll say the area behind these crates is the boys' and the one behind those is the girls'."

"Only thing is we'll have to take them with us when we move," Sean said.

"When we move?" Leslie asked, looking puzzled.

Patrick turned to her. "They're sure to search this place," he said. "But when they're on the way in, we'll slip down into the conduit and go the other way, to a room they've already searched. Right, Cap'n Doe?"

"You got it," Sean said. "And I'm trusting Nickie to let us know when a patrol is coming."

"Nobody'd better spill a chemical toilet on me," Nickie said in a grumpy voice. "We Russians consider that a great insult."

"We Poles aren't too crazy about it, either," Jenny told her.

Nickie's computer picked up the communication link. Most of the Doe Crew were grabbing some sleep when Nickie sought out Sean. "They know we're missing," she reported. "They're sending out calls for us. They'll be tracking the GPS bracelets when we don't respond."

It was 10:31 on the first day of their deadly serious game of hide-and-seek.

Nickie was asleep and Jenny was watching the computer when the search party found the locator bracelets and the note they had left. Nickie told the others that Dr. Simak had issued an order that they return to their dorms immediately.

They had lunch instead.

That afternoon the computer told them that a three-person search party was headed toward them. One by one they dropped into the conduit, Sean going last and latching the cover above him. They all wriggled and slid down to the first storage area as the search party walked right over them.

They had been careful. No one suffered from a toilet spill.

And it went like that for the next five days. . . .

11.1

Nickie's face was ghostly in the reflected glow of her tiny computer. Sean felt his heart racing. Part of it was the air—the atmosphere in the storage area was not as oxygen-rich as in the domes, and over the last few days they all had begun to feel headachy and groggy. Most of his discomfort, though, was nerves. He ached to ask Nickie what was happening, what decision had been reached, but they knew that adults were prowling the corridors again, making a desperate last sweep for the Asimov Project kids. Sean felt Jenny at his shoulder and could tell that she was just as tense as he was.

The others huddled together, shivering. Sean guessed it was eight or nine degrees in this storage compartment. "Is the heat completely off?" Jenny asked through chattering teeth.

"No," Sean whispered. "Just feels like it. But they can't let this storage area drop below freezing. There's medicine stored here. If it freezes, it would break the containers. This is as cold as it's going to get."

"Wish we could have some light," someone muttered. "Seems like we've been in the dark for—"

"Shh!" Nickie's quiet hiss.

Sean tried to force himself to breathe more normally. His arms were cold, his fingers nearly numb. He felt Mars was determined to freeze him into a solid block of ice. He wondered how many colonists were still searching for them. Not too many, with the *Argosy* racing to load any colonists who wanted to return to Earth. Soon there would be an anxious rush that would make searching impossible.

But—Sean swallowed hard—what if that wasn't happening at all? What if Dr. Simak had decided that the ship had to wait for the next departure window, in six months? There was no way his crew could hold out for that long.

"Okay," Nickie said in little more than a whisper. Sean sensed everyone leaning toward her, straining to hear. "Status report on the *Argosy* is finally coming through. The ship is loaded and—" Silence. Then, in an unbelieving voice: "Sean, they're taking a hundred and seventy-six passengers! That's all!"

"Has to be a mistake," someone said. "It's supposed to be over six hundred!"

Nickie didn't glance away from the tiny screen. "No mistake. Only a hundred and seventy-six volunteers. The rest have all decided to stay."

"My kind of people," Roger whispered. "The daring, dashing, brainless kind!"

Sean took a deep breath. "Most of them know there's not likely to be much on Earth to return to."

"Any word on the launch?" Jenny asked.

"*Argosy* is already cleared to leave orbit. Planet

command has just turned nav and command control over to the ship's crew."

"What if this is a trick?" asked Mickey Goldberg, his voice suspicious. "They may be trying to fake us out."

Sean shook his head before he realized that Mickey couldn't see him in the dark. "I don't think they realize we can tap into their net. If we didn't know what was going on, there'd be no point to a trick."

"They're about to launch!" Nickie said, her voice surprisingly loud in the darkness, edged with her excitement. "They can't turn back now. Less than a minute to go—"

Light flooded the compartment, cutting Nickie short, blinding them all.

"Here you are."

Sean shivered, not from the cold. Dr. Ellman had found them.

And he sounded far from happy.

The twenty young people of the Doe Crew stood miserably together, warmer than they had been in days but even more uncomfortable. The common area outside the Administration offices was hardly large enough for them to squeeze into, and with Dr. Ellman, Lieutenant Mpondo, and Dr. Simak glaring at them, the space seemed even smaller.

"You have caused us a great deal of trouble," Dr. Simak said, pacing as much as she could—two steps forward, two back.

Alex nudged Sean. "I wondered where you'd picked up that pacing habit," he whispered.

"You will be silent!" Behind Dr. Simak, Ellman could hardly contain his anger. His face was so red it was almost glowing. "What punishment do you recommend this time, *Doctor* Simak?" he demanded, his tone dripping with sarcasm. "It has to be more than confinement to quarters!"

Mpondo said mildly, "I don't think we can shoot them."

Dr. Simak closed her eyes. "Please! I'm tired and this is no time for bickering. Yes, Dr. Ellman, their punishment will be more severe than confinement to quarters. It will be confinement to the planet."

Ellman spluttered.

Dr. Simak raised a hand. "I didn't want these young people to face the uncertainty and danger that we have all agreed to face. However, that decision is now out of my hands." Looking directly at Sean, she continued. "We've heard from the L5 outposts and from the lunar colony. They have all agreed to hang on. There are fewer than ten thousand colonists in space, everything counted—space stations, lunar colony, and us. We're going to survive for as long as it takes. Reports from Earth are not encouraging. At best, it will be one year—one Martian year, mind you—until the *Magellan* rescue ship can hope to launch from lunar orbit to return to Mars. Then it will be months until it could possibly arrive here.

And even then—well, you know how limited that ship's capacity is. Like it or not, we're stranded here for the foreseeable future. I don't know how long it will take Earth to recover from this collapse, but until that time, our mission is simply to survive as best we can."

Mpondo added somberly, "The odds are against us. Unless we can tap new sources, we'll use up our water supply in a matter of months, even with full recycling. We have to protect our power generating facilities at all costs, or else we'll freeze to death. Food is marginal. If everything holds together, the greenhouses should barely provide for us. But one crop failure means we starve. We have no reserves, and we can't expect resupply from Earth."

"We know that," Sean blurted.

"And we don't care," added Jenny, stepping up to stand beside him. "It's our decision. We're going to stay."

"You will work," warned Mpondo. "We have to survive at all costs. That means no free rides. You'll all work harder than you ever have in your lives. You will continue your education, but you'll also have to pull a shift, just like every other colonist."

"That's fine," Sean said, his chin up. "We didn't expect anything else."

"Very well," Dr. Simak said. "Sean, you stay for a moment. The rest of you are dismissed. Get some food and some rest. You're going to need it."

"You can say anything to us that you're going to say to Sean," Mickey objected. "We're all in this together."

"I know that," Dr. Simak responded resignedly. "But Sean is in my foster care, and the rest of you are not. You're dismissed."

They filed out quietly, with Mpondo and Ellman the last to go. Sean met Ellman's glare as the heavyset man looked back over his shoulder. His sour expression promised that Sean in particular was going to have a hard time in the future.

"Come into my office, Sean," Amanda said at last. She pulled her chair from behind her desk and motioned Sean into the visitor's chair. She sat facing him, reached out, and took both of his hands in hers. "How did you know this was coming?" she asked.

Sean blinked. "The collapse on Earth?"

"You've talked about this before. You seemed to know it was coming even when the leaders on Earth were saying things were looking up. What told you that this disaster was about to happen?" Amanda stared intently into his eyes.

With a shrug, Sean said, "That's my only talent, I think. I can guess at trends and outcomes better than most people. For over two years now, I've been feeling that something drastic was going to happen on Earth, but I didn't know just what. That's why I wanted to be here." He paused and then added, "And I wanted to stay with you."

"Why did you talk the others into staying?"

"I didn't," Sean said. "When they found out I didn't plan to go back to Earth, they all decided to stay too. I didn't talk them into anything." He struggled for words. "This is more than a prank.

Look, the Asimov kids are all orphans. We don't have anything on Earth to return to. Marsport is our future, our hope of building something, maybe even of giving the human race a chance of surviving. I still don't know what's going to happen on Earth, whether it will pull through or. . . ." He shrugged again.

"None of us knows," Amanda said quietly. She sighed. "This is going to be very difficult for you and your friends, more difficult than anything you've ever done. I'm counting on you."

"On me?" Sean asked, surprised.

Amanda's expression was kind. "You do have talents, Sean, more than being able to assess probabilities. Maybe you didn't talk your friends into staying on Mars, but they stayed because of you. That's a talent. It's called leadership."

"I'm not a—"

"You are," she said simply. "The others feel it, even if they don't put it into words. Believe me, Sean, leadership is a tough job. Responsibility comes with it, and that can crush anyone who isn't prepared. If the others find the next months hard, you're going to find them all but impossible. We're living in a little pocket that human engineering has made habitable, but the rest of this planet will kill you."

Sean gave her a quizzical smile. "I know," he said. "Mars has a million ways of killing us. But that means we have to get very, very good at staying alive."

"Well put," said Dr. Simak dryly. "Now let's see if we can do that."

Sean nodded. His sense of doom, the sense that had so driven him when he was on Earth, had lifted. An odd kind of hope had replaced it—a hope colored with uncertainty, even a little fear. He didn't know what would happen now; maybe his feeling of impending catastrophe had even been a fluke. Maybe his cautious sense of optimism was wrong, and maybe disaster was waiting next week, or next month, or next season.

Maybe none of the Marsport colonists would get out of this alive.

Still, whatever happened, he was home.

And at the moment that made up for everything else.

Look for the second book in the MARS YEAR ONE trilogy

MARS
YEAR ONE
Missing!

Landslides, a deadly climate, and the increasingly unpredictable weather of Mars make survival nearly impossible, but the most immediate problem facing the Marsport colonists is the dwindling water supply. The group decides to construct an automated station in a rift valley where ice accumulated from the atmosphere will be melted and moved through warming pipelines to Marsport.

The kids of the Asimov Project participate in the work, but then a fierce storm hits and a team that includes Jenny is isolated and lost. Despite orders not to leave Marsport, Sean puts together a group of kids to go out and find the team. As the race to save the missing colonists becomes increasingly dangerous—and pits Sean against Amanda *and* the administration of the colony—Sean quickly learns that schisms within the social order are almost as deadly as Mars itself.

FALL 2004

MARS HAS A MILLION DIFFERENT WAYS TO KILL YOU. . . .

The year is 2085. Mars Experimental Station One, a colony built to test humans' ability to live in an alien and hostile environment, has been in existence for ten years. This functioning city of two thousand people includes only twenty teenagers, each hand selected from the billions on Earth as part of the controversial Asimov Project.

The Asimov teens each have reasons to doubt themselves and distrust each other. But one thing is certain: Mars offers them something Earth never could. When the existence of Marsport is threatened, the group must overcome their fears and join forces, for their survival depends on nothing less.

FOLLOW THE ADVENTURES OF THESE TEENS IN THE MARS YEAR ONE TRILOGY:

#1 MAROONED!
#2 MISSING!
#3 MARSQUAKE!

ALADDIN PAPERBACKS
SIMON & SCHUSTER CHILDREN'S DIVISION